John Galsworthy – Stories For My Family

John Galsworthy was born at Kingston Upon Thames in Surrey, England, on August 14th 1867 to a wealthy and well established family. His schooling was at Harrow and New College, Oxford before training as a barrister and being called to the bar in 1890. However, Law was not attractive to him and he travelled abroad becoming great friends with the novelist Joseph Conrad, then a first mate on a sailing ship.

In 1895 Galsworthy began an affair with Ada Nemesis Pearson Cooper, the wife of his cousin Major Arthur Galsworthy. The affair was kept a secret for 10 years till she at last divorced and they married on 23 September 1905.

Galsworthy first published in 1897 with a collection of short stories entitled "The Four Winds". For the next 7 years he published these and all works under his pen name John Sinjohn. It was only upon the death of his father and the publication of "The Island Pharisees" in 1904 that he published as John Galsworthy.

His first play, The Silver Box in 1906 was a success and was followed by "The Man of Property" later that same year and was the first in the Forsyte trilogy. Whilst today he is far more well know as a Nobel Prize winning novelist then he was considered a playwright dealing with social issues and the class system.

He is now far better known for his novels, particularly The Forsyte Saga, his trilogy about the eponymous family of the same name. These books, as with many of his other works, deal with social class, upper-middle class lives in particular. Although always sympathetic to his characters, he reveals their insular, snobbish, and somewhat greedy attitudes and suffocating moral codes. He is now viewed as one of the first from the Edwardian era to challenge some of the ideals of society depicted in the literature of Victorian England. Here we publish some of his short stories, dedicated to family members, from the turn of the Century when the Victorian era was changing to the Edwardian.

In his writings he campaigns for a variety of causes, including prison reform, women's rights, animal welfare, and the opposition of censorship as well as a recurring theme of an unhappy marriage from the women's side. During World War I he worked in a hospital in France as an orderly after being passed over for military service.

He was appointed to the Order of Merit in 1929, after earlier turning down a knighthood, and awarded the Nobel Prize in 1932 though he was too ill to attend.

John Galsworthy died from a brain tumour at his London home, Grove Lodge, Hampstead on January 31st 1933. In accordance with his will he was cremated at Woking with his ashes then being scattered over the South Downs from an aeroplane.

Index Of Contents

I - "MOOR, 20th July.

.... It is quiet here, sleepy, rather—a farm is never quiet; the sea, too, is only a quarter of a mile away, and when it's windy, the sound of it travels up the combe; for distraction, you must go four miles to Brixham or five to Kingswear, and you won't find much then. The farm lies in a sheltered spot, scooped, so to speak, high up the combe side—behind is a rise of fields, and beyond, a sweep of down. You have the feeling of being able to see quite far, which is misleading, as you soon find out if you walk. It is true Devon country-hills, hollows, hedge-banks, lanes dipping down into the earth or going up like the sides of houses, coppices, cornfields, and little streams wherever there's a place for one; but the downs along the cliff, all gorse and ferns, are wild. The combe ends in a sandy cove with black rock on one side, pinkish cliffs away to the headland on the other, and a coastguard station. Just now, with the harvest coming on, everything looks its richest, the apples ripening, the trees almost too green. It's very hot, still weather; the country and the sea seem to sleep in the sun. In front of the farm are half-a-dozen pines that look as if they had stepped out of another land, but all round the back is orchard as lush, and gnarled, and orthodox as any one could wish. The house, a long, white building with three levels of roof, and splashes of brown all over it, looks as if it might be growing down into the earth. It was freshly thatched two years ago—and that's all the newness there is about it; they say the front door, oak, with iron knobs, is three hundred years old at least. You can touch the ceilings with your hand. The windows certainly might be larger—a heavenly old place, though, with a flavour of apples, smoke, sweetbriar, bacon, honeysuckle, and age, all over it.

The owner is a man called John Ford, about seventy, and seventeen stone in weight—very big, on long legs, with a grey, stubbly beard, grey, watery eyes, short neck and purplish complexion; he is asthmatic, and has a very courteous, autocratic manner. His clothes are made of Harris tweed— except on Sundays, when he puts on black—a seal ring, and a thick gold cable chain. There's nothing mean or small about John Ford; I suspect him of a warm heart, but he doesn't let you know much about him. He's a north-country man by birth, and has been out in New Zealand all his life. This little Devonshire farm is all he has now. He had a large "station" in the North Island, and was much looked up to, kept open house, did everything, as one would guess, in a narrow-minded, large-handed way. He came to grief suddenly; I don't quite know how. I believe his only son lost money on the turf, and then, unable to face his father, shot himself; if you had seen John Ford, you could imagine that. His wife died, too, that year. He paid up to the last penny, and came home, to live on this farm. He told me the other night that he had only one relation in the world, his granddaughter, who lives here with him. Pasiance Voisey—old spelling for Patience, but they pronounce, it Pash-yence—is sitting out here with me at this moment on a sort of rustic loggia that opens into the orchard. Her sleeves are rolled up, and she's stripping currants, ready for black currant tea. Now and then she rests her elbows on the table, eats a berry, pouts her lips, and, begins again. She has a round, little face; a long, slender body; cheeks like poppies; a bushy mass of black-brown hair, and dark-brown, almost black, eyes; her nose is snub; her lips quick, red, rather full; all her motions quick and soft. She loves bright colours. She's rather like a little cat; sometimes she seems all sympathy, then in a moment as hard as tortoise-shell. She's all impulse; yet she doesn't like to show her feelings; I sometimes wonder whether she has any. She plays the violin.

It's queer to see these two together, queer and rather sad. The old man has a fierce tenderness for her that strikes into the very roots of him. I see him torn between it, and his cold north-country horror of his feelings; his life with her is an unconscious torture to him. She's a restless, chafing thing, demure enough one moment, then flashing out into mocking speeches or hard little laughs. Yet she's fond of him in her fashion; I saw her kiss him once when he was asleep. She obeys him generally—in a way as if she couldn't breathe while she was doing it. She's had a queer sort of education—history, geography, elementary mathematics, and nothing else; never been to school; had a few lessons on the violin, but has taught herself most of what she knows. She is well up in the lore of birds, flowers, and insects; has three cats, who follow her about; and is full of pranks. The other day she called out to me, "I've something for you. Hold out your hand and shut your eyes!" It was a large, black slug! She's the child of the old fellow's only daughter, who was sent home for schooling at Torquay, and made a runaway match with one Richard Voisey, a yeoman farmer, whom she met in the hunting-field. John Ford was furious—his ancestors, it appears, used to lead ruffians on the Cumberland side of the Border—he looked on "Squire" Rick Voisey as a cut below him. He was called "Squire," as far as I can make out, because he used to play cards every evening with a parson in the neighbourhood who went by the name of "Devil" Hawkins. Not that the Voisey stock is to be despised. They have had this farm since it was granted to one Richard Voysey by copy dated 8th September, 13 Henry VIII. Mrs. Hopgood, the wife of the bailiff—a dear, quaint, serene old soul with cheeks like a rosy, withered apple, and an unbounded love of Pasiance—showed me the very document.

"I kape it," she said. "Mr. Ford be tu proud—but other folks be proud tu. 'Tis a pra-aper old fam'ly: all the women is Margery, Pasiance, or Mary; all the men's Richards an' Johns an' Rogers; old as they apple-trees."

Rick Voisey was a rackety, hunting fellow, and "dipped" the old farm up to its thatched roof. John Ford took his revenge by buying up the mortgages, foreclosing, and commanding his daughter and Voisey to go on living here rent free; this they dutifully did until they were both killed in a dog-cart accident, eight years ago. Old Ford's financial smash came a year later, and since then he's lived here with Pasiance. I fancy it's the cross in her blood that makes her so restless, and irresponsible: if she had been all a native she'd have been happy enough here, or all a stranger like John Ford himself, but the two strains struggling for mastery seem to give her no rest. You'll think this a far-fetched theory, but I believe it to be the true one. She'll stand with lips pressed together, her arms folded tight across her narrow chest, staring as if she could see beyond the things round her; then something catches her attention, her eyes will grow laughing, soft, or scornful all in a minute! She's eighteen, perfectly fearless in a boat, but you can't get her to mount a horse—a sore subject with her grandfather, who spends most of his day on a lean, half-bred pony, that carries him like a feather, for all his weight.

They put me up here as a favour to Dan Treffry; there's an arrangement of L. s. d. with Mrs. Hopgood in the background. They aren't at all well off; this is the largest farm about, but it doesn't bring them in much. To look at John Ford, it seems incredible he should be short of money—he's too large.

We have family prayers at eight, then, breakfast—after that freedom for writing or anything else till supper and evening prayers. At midday one forages for oneself. On Sundays, two miles to church twice, or you get into John Ford's black books.... Dan Treffry himself is staying at Kingswear. He says he's made his pile; it suits him down here—like a sleep after years of being too wide-awake; he had a rough time in New Zealand, until that mine made his fortune. You'd hardly remember him; he reminds me of his uncle, old Nicholas Treffry; the same slow way of speaking, with a hesitation, and a trick of repeating your name with everything he says; left-handed too, and the same slow twinkle in his eyes. He has a dark, short beard, and red-brown cheeks; is a little bald on the temples, and a bit grey, but hard as iron. He rides over nearly every day, attended by a black spaniel with a wonderful nose and a horror of petticoats. He has told me lots of good stories of John Ford in the early squatter's times; his feats with horses live to this day; and he was through the Maori wars; as Dan says, "a man after Uncle Nic's own heart."

They are very good friends, and respect each other; Dan has a great admiration for the old man, but the attraction is Pasiance. He talks very little when she's in the room, but looks at her in a sidelong, wistful sort of way. Pasiance's conduct to him would be cruel in any one else, but in her, one takes it with a pinch of salt. Dan goes off, but turns up again as quiet and dogged as you please.

Last night, for instance, we were sitting in the loggia after supper. Pasiance was fingering the strings of her violin, and suddenly Dan (a bold thing for him) asked her to play.

"What!" she said, "before men? No, thank you!"

"Why not?"

"Because I hate them."

Down came John Ford's hand on the wicker table: "You forget yourself! Go to bed!"

She gave Dan a look, and went; we could hear her playing in her bedroom; it sounded like a dance of spirits; and just when one thought she had finished, out it would break again like a burst of laughter. Presently, John Ford begged our pardons ceremoniously, and stumped off indoors. The violin ceased; we heard his voice growling at her; down he came again. Just as he was settled in his chair there was a soft swish, and something dark came falling through the apple boughs. The violin! You should have seen his face! Dan would have picked the violin up, but the old man stopped him. Later, from my bedroom window, I saw John Ford come out and stand looking at the violin. He raised his foot as if to stamp on it. At last he picked it up, wiped it carefully, and took it in....

My room is next to hers. I kept hearing her laugh, a noise too as if she were dragging things about the room. Then I fell asleep, but woke with a start, and went to the window for a breath of fresh air. Such a black, breathless night! Nothing to be seen but the twisted, blacker branches; not the faintest stir of leaves, no sound but muffled grunting from the cowhouse, and now and then a faint sigh. I had the queerest feeling of unrest and fear, the last thing to expect on such a night. There is something here that's disturbing; a sort of suppressed struggle. I've never in my life seen anything so irresponsible as this girl, or so uncompromising as the old man; I keep thinking of the way he wiped that violin. It's just as if a spark would set everything in a blaze. There's a menace of tragedy—or—perhaps it's only the heat, and too much of Mother Hopgood's crame....

II - "Tuesday.

.... I've made a new acquaintance. I was lying in the orchard, and presently, not seeing me, he came along—a man of middle height, with a singularly good balance, and no lumber—rather old blue clothes, a flannel shirt, a dull red necktie, brown shoes, a cap with a leather peak pushed up on the forehead. Face long and narrow, bronzed with a kind of pale burnt-in brownness; a good forehead. A brown moustache, beard rather pointed, blackening about the cheeks; his chin not visible, but from the beard's growth must be big; mouth I should judge sensuous. Nose straight and blunt; eyes grey, with an upward look, not exactly frank, because defiant; two parallel furrows down each cheek, one from the inner corner of the eye, one from the nostril; age perhaps thirty-five. About the face, attitude, movements, something immensely vital, adaptable, daring, and unprincipled.

He stood in front of the loggia, biting his fingers, a kind of nineteenth-century buccaneer, and I wondered what he was doing in this galley. They say you can tell a man of Kent or a Somersetshire man; certainly you can tell a Yorkshire man, and this fellow could only have been a man of Devon, one of the two main types found in this county. He whistled; and out came Pasiance in a geranium-coloured dress, looking like some tall poppy—you know the slight droop of a poppy's head, and the way the wind sways its stem.... She is a human poppy, her fuzzy dark hair is like a poppy's lustreless black heart, she has a poppy's tantalising attraction and repulsion, something fatal, or rather fateful. She came walking up to my new friend, then caught sight of me, and stopped dead.

"That," she said to me, "is Zachary Pearse. This," she said to him, "is our lodger." She said it with a wonderful soft malice. She wanted to scratch me, and she scratched. Half an hour later I was in the yard, when up came this fellow Pearse.

"Glad to know you," he said, looking thoughtfully at the pigs.

"You're a writer, aren't you?"

"A sort of one," I said.

"If by any chance," he said suddenly, "you're looking for a job, I could put something in your way. Walk down to the beach with me, and I'll tell you; my boat's at anchor, smartest little craft in these parts."

It was very hot, and I had no desire whatever to go down to the beach—I went, all the same. We had not gone far when John Ford and Dan Treffry came into the lane. Our friend seemed a little disconcerted, but soon recovered himself. We met in the middle of the lane, where there was hardly room to pass. John Ford, who looked very haughty, put on his pince-nez and stared at Pearse.

"Good-day!" said Pearse; "fine weather! I've been up to ask Pasiance to come for a sail. Wednesday we thought, weather permitting; this gentleman's coming. Perhaps you'll come too, Mr. Treffry. You've never seen my place. I'll give you lunch, and show you my father. He's worth a couple of hours' sail any day." It was said in such an odd way that one couldn't resent his impudence. John Ford was seized with a fit of wheezing, and seemed on the eve of an explosion; he glanced at me, and checked himself.

"You're very good," he said icily; "my granddaughter has other things to do. You, gentlemen, will please yourselves"; and, with a very slight bow, he went stumping on to the house. Dan looked at me, and I looked at him.

"You'll come?" said Pearse, rather wistfully. Dan stammered: "Thank you, Mr. Pearse; I'm a better man on a horse than in a boat, but—thank you." Cornered in this way, he's a shy, soft-hearted being. Pearse smiled his thanks. "Wednesday, then, at ten o'clock; you shan't regret it."

"Pertinacious beggar!" I heard Dan mutter in his beard; and found myself marching down the lane again by Pearse's side. I asked him what he was good enough to mean by saying I was coming, without having asked me. He answered, unabashed:

"You see, I'm not friends with the old man; but I knew he'd not be impolite to you, so I took the liberty."

He has certainly a knack of turning one's anger to curiosity. We were down in the combe now; the tide was running out, and the sand all little, wet, shining ridges. About a quarter of a mile out lay a cutter, with her tan sail half down, swinging to the swell. The sunlight was making the pink cliffs glow in the most wonderful way; and shifting in bright patches over the sea like moving shoals of goldfish. Pearse perched himself on his dinghy, and looked out under his hand. He seemed lost in admiration.

"If we could only net some of those spangles," he said, "an' make gold of 'em! No more work then."

"It's a big job I've got on," he said presently; "I'll tell you about it on Wednesday. I want a journalist."

"But I don't write for the papers," I said; "I do other sort of work. My game is archaeology."

"It doesn't matter," he said, "the more imagination the better. It'd be a thundering good thing for you."

His assurance was amazing, but it was past supper-time, and hunger getting the better of my curiosity, I bade him good-night. When I looked back, he was still there, on the edge of his boat, gazing at the sea. A queer sort of bird altogether, but attractive somehow.

Nobody mentioned him that evening; but once old Ford, after staring a long time at Pasiance, muttered a propos of nothing, "Undutiful children!" She was softer than usual; listening quietly to our talk, and smiling when spoken to. At bedtime she went up to her grand-father, without waiting for the usual command, "Come and kiss me, child."

Dan did not stay to supper, and he has not been here since. This morning I asked Mother Hopgood who Zachary Pearse was. She's a true Devonian; if there's anything she hates, it is to be committed to a definite statement. She ambled round her answer, and at last told me that he was "son of old Cap'en Jan Pearse to Black Mill. 'Tes an old family to Dartymouth an' Plymouth," she went on in a communicative outburst. "They du say Francis Drake tuke five o' they Pearses with 'en to fight the Spaniards. At least that's what I've heard Mr. Zachary zay; but Ha-apgood can tell yu." Poor Hopgood, the amount of information she saddles him with in the course of the day! Having given me thus to understand that she had run dry, she at once went on:

"Cap'en Jan Pearse made a dale of ventures. He's old now—they du say nigh an 'undred. Ha-apgood can tell yu."

"But the son, Mrs. Hopgood?"

Her eyes twinkled with sudden shrewdness: She hugged herself placidly.

"An' what would yu take for dinner to-day? There's duck; or yu might like 'toad in the hole,' with an apple tart; or then, there's—Well! we'll see what we can du like." And off she went, without waiting for my answer.

To-morrow is Wednesday. I shan't be sorry to get another look at this fellow Pearse....

III - "Friday, 29th July.

.... Why do you ask me so many questions, and egg me on to write about these people instead of minding my business? If you really want to hear, I'll tell you of Wednesday's doings.

It was a splendid morning; and Dan turned up, to my surprise—though I might have known that when he says a thing, he does it. John Ford came out to shake hands with him, then, remembering why he had come, breathed loudly, said nothing, and went in again. Nothing was to be seen of Pasiance, and we went down to the beach together.

"I don't like this fellow Pearse, George," Dan said to me on the way; "I was fool enough to say I'd go, and so I must, but what's he after? Not the man to do things without a reason, mind you."

I remarked that we should soon know.

"I'm not so sure—queer beggar; I never look at him without thinking of a pirate."

The cutter lay in the cove as if she had never moved. There too was Zachary Pearse seated on the edge of his dinghy.

"A five-knot breeze," he said, "I'll run you down in a couple of hours." He made no inquiry about Pasiance, but put us into his cockleshell and pulled for the cutter. A lantern-Jawed fellow, named Prawle, with a spiky, prominent beard, long, clean-shaven upper lip, and tanned complexion—a regular hard-weather bird—received us.

The cutter was beautifully clean; built for a Brixham trawler, she still had her number—DH 113—uneffaced. We dived into a sort of cabin, airy, but dark, fitted with two bunks and a small table, on which stood some bottles of stout; there were lockers, too, and pegs for clothes. Prawle, who showed us round, seemed very proud of a steam contrivance for hoisting sails. It was some minutes before we came on deck again; and there, in the dinghy, being pulled towards the cutter, sat Pasiance.

"If I'd known this," stammered Dan, getting red, "I wouldn't have come." She had outwitted us, and there was nothing to be done.

It was a very pleasant sail. The breeze was light from the south-east, the sun warm, the air soft. Presently Pasiance began singing:

"Columbus is dead and laid in his grave, Oh! heigh-ho! and laid in his grave; Over his head the apple-trees wave Oh! heigh-ho! the apple-trees wave....

"The apples are ripe and ready to fall, Oh! heigh-ho! and ready to fall; There came an old woman and gathered them all, Oh! heigh-ho! and gathered them all....

"The apples are gathered, and laid on the shelf, Oh! heigh-ho! and laid on the shelf; If you want any more, you must sing for yourself, Oh! heigh-ho! and sing for yourself."

Her small, high voice came to us in trills and spurts, as the wind let it, like the singing of a skylark lost in the sky. Pearse went up to her and whispered something. I caught a glimpse of her face like a startled wild creature's; shrinking, tossing her hair, laughing, all in the same breath. She wouldn't sing again, but crouched in the bows with her chin on her hands, and the sun falling on one cheek, round, velvety, red as a peach....

We passed Dartmouth, and half an hour later put into a little wooded bay. On a low reddish cliff was a house hedged round by pine-trees. A bit of broken jetty ran out from the bottom of the cliff. We hooked on to this, and landed. An ancient, fish-like man came slouching down and took charge of the cutter. Pearse led us towards the house, Pasiance following mortally shy all of a sudden.

The house had a dark, overhanging thatch of the rush reeds that grow in the marshes hereabouts; I remember nothing else remarkable. It was neither old, nor new; neither beautiful, nor exactly ugly; neither clean, nor entirely squalid; it perched there with all its windows over the sea, turning its back contemptuously on the land.

Seated in a kind of porch, beside an immense telescope, was a very old man in a panama hat, with a rattan cane. His pure-white beard and moustache, and almost black eyebrows, gave a very singular, piercing look to his little, restless, dark-grey eyes; all over his mahogany cheeks and neck was a network of fine wrinkles. He sat quite upright, in the full sun, hardly blinking.

"Dad!" said Zachary, "this is Pasiance Voisey." The old man turned his eyes on her and muttered, "How do you do, ma'am?" then took no further notice. And Pasiance, who seemed to resent this, soon slipped away and went wandering about amongst the pines. An old woman brought some plates and bottles and laid them casually on a table; and we sat round the figure of old Captain Pearse without a word, as if we were all under a spell.

Before lunch there was a little scene between Zachary Pearse and Dan, as to which of them should summon Pasiance. It ended in both going, and coming back without her. She did not want any lunch, would stay where she was amongst the pines.

For lunch we had chops, wood-pigeons, mushrooms, and mulberry preserve, and drank wonderful Madeira out of common wine-glasses. I asked the old man where he got it; he gave me a queer look, and answered with a little bow:

"Stood me in tu shillin' the bottle, an' the country got nothing out of it, sir. In the early Thirties; tu shillin' the bottle; there's no such wine nowadays and," he added, looking at Zachary, "no such men."

Zachary smiled and said: "You did nothing so big, dad, as what I'm after, now!"

The old man's eyes had a sort of disdain in them.

"You're going far, then, in the Pied Witch, Zack?"

"I am," said Zachary.

"And where might yu be goin' in that old trampin' smut factory?"

"Morocco."

"Heu!" said the old man, "there's nothing there; I know that coast, as I know the back o' my hand." He stretched out a hand covered with veins and hair.

Zachary began suddenly to pour out a flood of words:

"Below Mogador—a fellow there—friend of mine—two years ago now. Concessions—trade—gunpowder—cruisers—feuds—money— chiefs—Gatling guns—Sultan—rifles—rebellion—gold." He detailed a reckless, sordid, bold scheme, which, on the pivot of a trading venture, was intended to spin a whole wheel of political convulsions.

"They'll never let you get there," said old Pearse.

"Won't they?" returned Zachary. "Oh yes, they will, an' when I leave, there'll be another dynasty, and I'll be a rich man."

"Yu'll never leave," answered the old man.

Zachary took out a sheet of paper covered with figures. He had worked the whole thing out. So much—equipment, so much—trade, so much—concessions, so much—emergencies. "My last mag!" he ended, "a thousand short; the ship's ready, and if I'm not there within a month my chance is as good as gone."

This was the pith of his confidences—an appeal for money, and we all looked as men will when that crops up.

"Mad!" muttered the old man, looking at the sea.

"No," said Zachary. That one word was more eloquent than all the rest of his words put together. This fellow is no visionary. His scheme may be daring, and unprincipled, but—he knows very well what he's about.

"Well!" said old Pearse, "you shall have five 'undred of my money, if it's only to learn what yu're made of. Wheel me in!" Zachary wheeled him into the house, but soon came back.

"The old man's cheque for five hundred pounds!" he said, holding it up. "Mr. Treffry, give me another, and you shall have a third of the profits."

I expected Dan to give a point-blank refusal. But he only asked:

"Would that clear you for starting?"

"With that," said Zachary, "I can get to sea in a fortnight."

"Good!" Dan said slowly. "Give me a written promise! To sea in fourteen days and my fair share on the five hundred pounds—no more—no less."

Again I thought Pearse would have jumped at this, but he leaned his chin on his hand, and looked at Dan, and Dan looked at him. While they were staring at each other like this, Pasiance came up with a kitten.

"See!" she said, "isn't it a darling?" The kitten crawled and clawed its way up behind her neck. I saw both men's eyes as they looked at Pasiance, and suddenly understood what they were at. The kitten rubbed itself against Pasiance's cheek, overbalanced, and fell, clawing, down her dress. She caught it up and walked away. Some one, I don't know which of us, sighed, and Pearse cried "Done!"

The bargain had been driven.

"Good-bye, Mr. Pearse," said Dan; "I guess that's all I'm wanted for. I'll find my pony waiting in the village. George, you'll see Pasiance home?"

We heard the hoofs of his pony galloping down the road; Pearse suddenly excused himself, and disappeared.

This venture of his may sound romantic and absurd, but it's matter-of-fact enough. He's after L. s. d.! Shades of Drake, Raleigh, Hawkins, Oxenham! The worm of suspicion gnaws at the rose of romance. What if those fellows, too, were only after L. s. d....?

I strolled into the pine-wood. The earth there was covered like a bee's body with black and gold stripes; there was the blue sea below, and white, sleepy clouds, and bumble-bees booming above the heather; it was all softness, a summer's day in Devon. Suddenly I came on Pearse standing at the edge of the cliff with Pasiance sitting in a little hollow below, looking up at him. I heard him say:

"Pasiance—Pasiance!" The sound of his voice, and the sight of her soft, wondering face made me furious. What business has she with love, at her age? What business have they with each other?

He told me presently that she had started off for home, and drove me to the ferry, behind an old grey pony. On the way he came back to his offer of the other day.

"Come with me," he said. "It doesn't do to neglect the Press; you can see the possibilities. It's one of the few countries left. If I once get this business started you don't know where it's going to stop. You'd have free passage everywhere, and whatever you like in reason."

I answered as rudely as I could—but by no means as rudely as I wanted—that his scheme was mad. As a matter of fact, it's much too sane for me; for, whatever the body of a scheme, its soul is the fibre of the schemer.

"Think of it," he urged, as if he could see into me. "You can make what you like of it. Press paragraphs, of course. But that's mechanical; why, even I could do it, if I had time. As for the rest, you'll be as free—as free as a man."

There, in five words of one syllable, is the kernel of this fellow Pearse—"As free as a man!" No rule, no law, not even the mysterious shackles that bind men to their own self-respects! "As free as a man!" No ideals; no principles; no fixed star for his worship; no coil he can't slide out of! But the fellow has the tenacity of one of the old Devon mastiffs, too. He wouldn't take "No" for an answer.

"Think of it," he said; "any day will do—I've got a fortnight.... Look! there she is!" I thought that he meant Pasiance; but it was an old steamer, sluggish and black in the blazing sun of mid-stream, with a yellow-and-white funnel, and no sign of life on her decks.

"That's her—the Pied Witch! Do her twelve knots; you wouldn't think it! Well! good-evening! You'd better come. A word to me at any time. I'm going aboard now."

As I was being ferried across I saw him lolling in the stern-sheets of a little boat, the sun crowning his straw hat with glory.

I came on Pasiance, about a mile up the road, sitting in the hedge. We walked on together between the banks—Devonshire banks, as high as houses, thick with ivy and ferns, bramble and hazel boughs, and honeysuckle.

"Do you believe in a God?" she said suddenly.

"Grandfather's God is simply awful. When I'm playing the fiddle, I can feel God; but grandfather's is such a stuffy God—you know what I mean: the sea, the wind, the trees, colours too—they make one feel. But I don't believe that life was meant to 'be good' in. Isn't there anything better than being good? When I'm 'good,' I simply feel wicked." She reached up, caught a flower from the hedge, and slowly tore its petals.

"What would you do," she muttered, "if you wanted a thing, but were afraid of it? But I suppose you're never afraid!" she added, mocking me. I admitted that I was sometimes afraid, and often afraid of being afraid.

"That's nice! I'm not afraid of illness, nor of grandfather, nor of his God; but—I want to be free. If you want a thing badly, you're afraid about it."

I thought of Zachary Pearse's words, "free as a man."

"Why are you looking at me like that?" she said.

I stammered: "What do you mean by freedom?"

"Do you know what I shall do to-night?" she answered. "Get out of my window by the apple-tree, and go to the woods, and play!"

We were going down a steep lane, along the side of a wood, where there's always a smell of sappy leaves, and the breath of the cows that come close to the hedge to get the shade.

There was a cottage in the bottom, and a small boy sat outside playing with a heap of dust.

"Hallo, Johnny!" said Pasiance. "Hold your leg out and show this man your bad place!" The small boy undid a bandage round his bare and dirty little leg, and proudly revealed a sore.

"Isn't it nasty?" cried Pasiance ruefully, tying up the bandage again; "poor little feller! Johnny, see what I've brought you!" She produced from her pocket a stick of chocolate, the semblance of a soldier made of sealing-wax and worsted, and a crooked sixpence.

It was a new glimpse of her. All the way home she was telling me the story of little Johnny's family; when she came to his mother's death, she burst out: "A beastly shame, wasn't it, and they're so poor; it might just as well have been somebody else. I like poor people, but I hate rich ones—stuck-up beasts."

Mrs. Hopgood was looking over the gate, with her cap on one side, and one of Pasiance's cats rubbing itself against her skirts. At the sight of us she hugged herself.

"Where's grandfather?" asked Pasiance. The old lady shook her head.

"Is it a row?" Mrs. Hopgood wriggled, and wriggled, and out came:

"Did you get yure tay, my pretty? No? Well, that's a pity; yu'll be falin' low-like."

Pasiance tossed her head, snatched up the cat, and ran indoors. I remained staring at Mrs. Hopgood.

"Dear-dear," she clucked, "poor lamb. So to spake it's—" and she blurted out suddenly, "chuckin' full of wra-ath, he is. Well, there!"

My courage failed that evening. I spent it at the coastguard station, where they gave me bread and cheese and some awful cider. I passed the kitchen as I came back. A fire was still burning there, and two figures, misty in the darkness, flitted about with stealthy laughter like spirits afraid of being detected in a carnal-meal. They were Pasiance and Mrs. Hopgood; and so charming was the smell of eggs and bacon, and they had such an air of tender enjoyment of this dark revel, that I stifled many pangs, as I crept hungry up to bed.

In the middle of the night I woke and heard what I thought was screaming; then it sounded like wind in trees, then like the distant shaking of a tambourine, with the high singing of a human voice. Suddenly it stopped—two long notes came wailing out like sobs—then utter stillness; and though I listened for an hour or more there was no other sound ....

IV - "4th August.

.... For three days after I wrote last, nothing at all happened here. I spent the mornings on the cliff reading, and watching the sun-sparks raining on the sea. It's grand up there with the gorse all round, the gulls basking on the rocks, the partridges calling in the corn, and now and then a young hawk overhead. The afternoons I spent out in the orchard. The usual routine goes on at the farm all the time—cow-milking, bread-baking, John Ford riding in and out, Pasiance in her garden stripping lavender, talking to the farm hands; and the smell of clover, and cows and hay; the sound of hens and pigs and pigeons, the soft drawl of voices, the dull thud of the farm carts; and day by day the apples getting redder. Then, last Monday, Pasiance was away from sunrise till sunset—nobody saw her go—nobody knew where she had gone. It was a wonderful, strange day, a sky of silver-grey and blue, with a drift of wind-clouds, all the trees sighing a little, the sea heaving in a long, low swell, the animals restless, the birds silent, except the gulls with their old man's laughter and kitten's mewing.

A something wild was in the air; it seemed to sweep across the downs and combe, into the very house, like a passionate tune that comes drifting to your ears when you're sleepy. But who would have thought the absence of that girl for a few hours could have wrought such havoc! We were like uneasy spirits; Mrs. Hopgood's apple cheeks seemed positively to wither before one's eyes. I came across a dairymaid and farm hand discussing it stolidly with very downcast faces. Even Hopgood, a hard-bitten fellow with immense shoulders, forgot his imperturbability so far as to harness his horse, and depart on what he assured me was "just a wild-guse chaace." It was long before John Ford gave signs of noticing that anything was wrong, but late in the afternoon I found him sitting with his hands on his knees, staring straight before him. He rose heavily when he saw me, and stalked out. In the evening, as I was starting for the coastguard station to ask for help to search the cliff, Pasiance appeared, walking as if she could hardly drag one leg after the other. Her cheeks were crimson; she was biting her lips to keep tears of sheer fatigue out of her eyes. She passed me in the doorway without a word. The anxiety he had gone through seemed to forbid the old man from speaking. He just came forward, took her face in his hands, gave it a great kiss, and walked away. Pasiance dropped on the floor in the dark passage, and buried her face on her arms. "Leave me alone!" was all she would say. After a bit she dragged herself upstairs. Presently Mrs. Hopgood came to me.

"Not a word out of her—an' not a bite will she ate, an' I had a pie all ready—scrumptious. The good Lord knows the truth—she asked for brandy; have you any brandy, sir? Ha-apgood'e don't drink it, an' Mister Ford 'e don't allaow for anything but caowslip wine."

I had whisky.

The good soul seized the flask, and went off hugging it. She returned it to me half empty.

"Lapped it like a kitten laps milk. I misdaoubt it's straong, poor lamb, it lusened 'er tongue praaperly. 'I've a-done it,' she says to me, 'Mums-I've a-done it,' an' she laughed like a mad thing; and then, sir, she cried, an' kissed me, an' pusshed me thru the door. Gude Lard! What is 't she's a-done...?"

It rained all the next day and the day after. About five o'clock yesterday the rain ceased; I started off to Kingswear on Hopgood's nag to see Dan Treffry. Every tree, bramble, and fern in the lanes was dripping water; and every bird singing from the bottom of his heart. I thought of Pasiance all the time. Her absence that day was still a mystery; one never ceased asking oneself what she had done. There are people who never grow up—they have no right to do things. Actions have consequences— and children have no business with consequences.

Dan was out. I had supper at the hotel, and rode slowly home. In the twilight stretches of the road, where I could touch either bank of the lane with my whip, I thought of nothing but Pasiance and her grandfather; there was something in the half light suited to wonder and uncertainty. It had fallen dark before I rode into the straw-yard. Two young bullocks snuffled at me, a sleepy hen got up and ran off with a tremendous shrieking. I stabled the horse, and walked round to the back. It was pitch black under the apple-trees, and the windows were all darkened. I stood there a little, everything smelled so delicious after the rain; suddenly I had the uncomfortable feeling that I was being watched. Have you ever felt like that on a dark night? I called out at last: "Is any one there?" Not a sound! I walked to the gate-nothing! The trees still dripped with tiny, soft, hissing sounds, but that was all. I slipped round to the front, went in, barricaded the door, and groped up to bed. But I couldn't sleep. I lay awake a long while; dozed at last, and woke with a jump. A stealthy murmur of smothered voices was going on quite close somewhere. It stopped. A minute passed; suddenly came the soft thud as of something falling. I sprang out of bed and rushed to the window. Nothing—but in the distance something that sounded like footsteps. An owl hooted; then clear as crystal, but quite low, I heard Pasiance singing in her room:

"The apples are ripe and ready to fall. Oh! heigh-ho! and ready to fall."

I ran to her door and knocked.

"What is it?" she cried.

"Is anything the matter?"

"Matter?"

"Is anything the matter?"

"Ha-ha-ha-ha! Good-night!" then quite low, I heard her catch her breath, hard, sharply. No other answer, no other sound.

I went to bed and lay awake for hours....

This evening Dan came; during supper he handed Pasiance a roll of music; he had got it in Torquay. The shopman, he said, had told him that it was a "corker."

It was Bach's "Chaconne." You should have seen her eyes shine, her fingers actually tremble while she turned over the pages. Seems odd to think of her worshipping at the shrine of Bach as odd as to think of a wild colt running of its free will into the shafts; but that's just it with her you can never tell. "Heavenly!" she kept saying.

John Ford put down his knife and fork.

"Heathenish stuff!" he muttered, and suddenly thundered out, "Pasiance!"

She looked up with a start, threw the music from her, and resumed her place.

During evening prayers, which follow every night immediately on food, her face was a study of mutiny. She went to bed early. It was rather late when we broke up—for once old Ford had been talking of his squatter's life. As we came out, Dan held up his hand. A dog was barking. "It's Lass," he said. "She'll wake Pasiance."

The spaniel yelped furiously. Dan ran out to stop her. He was soon back.

"Somebody's been in the orchard, and gone off down to the cove." He ran on down the path. I, too, ran, horribly uneasy. In front, through the darkness, came the spaniel's bark; the lights of the coastguard station faintly showed. I was first on the beach; the dog came to me at once, her tail almost in her mouth from apology. There was the sound of oars working in rowlocks; nothing visible but the feathery edges of the waves. Dan said behind, "No use! He's gone." His voice sounded hoarse, like that of a man choking with passion.

"George," he stammered, "it's that blackguard. I wish I'd put a bullet in him." Suddenly a light burned up in the darkness on the sea, seemed to swing gently, and vanished. Without another word we went back up the hill. John Ford stood at the gate motionless, indifferent—nothing had dawned on him as yet. I whispered to Dan, "Let it alone!"

"No," he said, "I'm going to show you." He struck a match, and slowly hunted the footsteps in the wet grass of the orchard. "Look—here!"

He stopped under Pasiance's window and swayed the match over the ground. Clear as daylight were the marks of some one who had jumped or fallen. Dan held the match over his head.

"And look there!" he said. The bough of an apple-tree below the window was broken. He blew the match out.

I could see the whites of his eyes, like an angry animal's.

"Drop it, Dan!" I said.

He turned on his heel suddenly, and stammered out, "You're right."

But he had turned into John Ford's arms.

The old man stood there like some great force, darker than the darkness, staring up at the window, as though stupefied. We had not a word to say. He seemed unconscious of our presence. He turned round, and left us standing there.

"Follow him!" said Dan. "Follow him—by God! it's not safe."

We followed. Bending, and treading heavily, he went upstairs. He struck a blow on Pasiance's door. "Let me in!" he said. I drew Dan into my bedroom. The key was slowly turned, her door was flung open, and there she stood in her dressing-gown, a candle in her hand, her face crimson, and oh! so young, with its short, crisp hair and round cheeks. The old man—like a giant in front of her—raised his hands, and laid them on her shoulders.

"What's this? You—you've had a man in your room?"

Her eyes did not drop.

"Yes," she said. Dan gave a groan.

"Who?"

"Zachary Pearse," she answered in a voice like a bell.

He gave her one awful shake, dropped his hands, then raised them as though to strike her. She looked him in the eyes; his hands dropped, and he too groaned. As far as I could see, her face never moved.

"I'm married to him," she said, "d' you hear? Married to him. Go out of my room!" She dropped the candle on the floor at his feet, and slammed the door in his face. The old man stood for a minute as though stunned, then groped his way downstairs.

"Dan," I said, "is it true?"

"Ah!" he answered, "it's true; didn't you hear her?"

I was glad I couldn't see his face.

"That ends it," he said at last; "there's the old man to think of."

"What will he do?"

"Go to the fellow this very night." He seemed to have no doubt. Trust one man of action to know another.

I muttered something about being an outsider—wondered if there was anything I could do to help.

"Well," he said slowly, "I don't know that I'm anything but an outsider now; but I'll go along with him, if he'll have me."

He went downstairs. A few minutes later they rode out from the straw-yard. I watched them past the line of hayricks, into the blacker shadows of the pines, then the tramp of hoofs began to fail in the darkness, and at last died away.

I've been sitting here in my bedroom writing to you ever since, till my candle's almost gone. I keep thinking what the end of it is to be; and reproaching myself for doing nothing. And yet, what could I have done? I'm sorry for her—sorrier than I can say. The night is so quiet—I haven't heard a sound; is she asleep, awake, crying, triumphant?

It's four o'clock; I've been asleep.

They're back. Dan is lying on my bed. I'll try and tell you his story as near as I can, in his own words.

"We rode," he said, "round the upper way, keeping out of the lanes, and got to Kingswear by half-past eleven. The horse-ferry had stopped running, and we had a job to find any one to put us over. We hired the fellow to wait for us, and took a carriage at the 'Castle.' Before we got to Black Mill it was nearly one, pitch-dark. With the breeze from the southeast, I made out he should have been in an hour or more. The old man had never spoken to me once: and before we got there I had begun to hope we shouldn't find the fellow after all. We made the driver pull up in the road, and walked round and round, trying to find the door. Then some one cried, 'Who are you?'

"'John Ford.'

"'What do you want?' It was old Pearse.

"'To see Zachary Pearse.'

"The long window out of the porch where we sat the other day was open, and in we went. There was a door at the end of the room, and a light coming through. John Ford went towards it; I stayed out in the dark.

"'Who's that with you?'

"'Mr. Treffry.'

"'Let him come in!' I went in. The old fellow was in bed, quite still on his pillows, a candle by his side; to look at him you'd think nothing of him but his eyes were alive. It was queer being there with those two old men!"

Dan paused, seemed to listen, then went on doggedly.

"'Sit down, gentleman,' said old Pearse. 'What may you want to see my son for?' John Ford begged his pardon, he had something to say, he said, that wouldn't wait.

"They were very polite to one another," muttered Dan ....

"'Will you leave your message with me?' said Pearse.

"'What I have to say to your son is private.'

"'I'm his father.'

"'I'm my girl's grandfather; and her only stand-by.'

"'Ah!' muttered old Pearse, 'Rick Voisey's daughter?'

"'I mean to see your son.'

"Old Pearse smiled. Queer smile he's got, sort of sneering sweet.

"'You can never tell where Zack may be,' he said. 'You think I want to shield him. You're wrong; Zack can take care of himself.'

"'Your son's here!' said John Ford. 'I know.' Old Pearse gave us a very queer look.

"'You come into my house like thieves in the night,' he said, 'and give me the lie, do you?'

"'Your son came to my child's room like a thief in the night; it's for that I want to see him,' and then," said Dan, "there was a long silence. At last Pearse said:

"'I don't understand; has he played the blackguard?'

"John Ford answered, 'He's married her, or, before God, I'd kill him.'

"Old Pearse seemed to think this over, never moving on his pillows. 'You don't know Zack,' he said; 'I'm sorry for you, and I'm sorry for Rick Voisey's daughter; but you don't know Zack.'

"'Sorry!' groaned out John Ford; 'he's stolen my child, and I'll punish him.'

"'Punish!' cried old Pearse, 'we don't take punishment, not in my family.'

"'Captain Jan Pearse, as sure as I stand here, you and your breed will get your punishment of God.' Old Pearse smiled.

"'Mr. John Ford, that's as may be; but sure as I lie here we won't take it of you. You can't punish unless you make to feel, and that you can't du.'"

And that is truth!

Dan went on again:

"'You won't tell me where your son is!' but old Pearse never blinked.

"'I won't,' he said, 'and now you may get out. I lie here an old man alone, with no use to my legs, night on night, an' the house open; any rapscallion could get in; d' ye think I'm afraid of you?'

"We were beat; and walked out without a word. But that old man; I've thought of him a lot—ninety-two, and lying there. Whatever he's been, and they tell you rum things of him, whatever his son may be, he's a man. It's not what he said, nor that there was anything to be afraid of just then, but somehow it's the idea of the old chap lying there. I don't ever wish to see a better plucked one...."

We sat silent after that; out of doors the light began to stir among the leaves. There were all kinds of rustling sounds, as if the world were turning over in bed.

Suddenly Dan said:

"He's cheated me. I paid him to clear out and leave her alone. D' you think she's asleep?" He's made no appeal for sympathy, he'd take pity for an insult; but he feels it badly.

"I'm tired as a cat," he said at last, and went to sleep on my bed.

It's broad daylight now; I too am tired as a cat....

V - "Saturday, 6th August.

.... I take up my tale where I left off yesterday.... Dan and I started as soon as we could get Mrs. Hopgood to give us coffee. The old lady was more tentative, more undecided, more pouncing, than I had ever seen her. She was manifestly uneasy: Ha-apgood—who "don't slape" don't he, if snores are any criterion—had called out in the night, "Hark to th' 'arses' 'oofs!" Had we heard them? And where might we be going then? 'Twas very earrly to start, an' no breakfast. Haapgood had said it was goin' to shaowerr. Miss Pasiance was not to 'er violin yet, an' Mister Ford 'e kept 'is room. Was it?—would there be—? "Well, an' therr's an 'arvest bug; 'tis some earrly for they!" Wonderful how she pounces on all such creatures, when I can't even see them. She pressed it absently between finger and thumb, and began manoeuvring round another way. Long before she had reached her point, we had gulped down our coffee, and departed. But as we rode out she came at a run, holding her skirts high with either hand, raised her old eyes bright and anxious in their setting of fine wrinkles, and said:

"'Tidden sorrow for her?"

A shrug of the shoulders was all the answer she got. We rode by the lanes; through sloping farmyards, all mud and pigs, and dirty straw, and farmers with clean-shaven upper lips and whiskers under the chin; past fields of corn, where larks were singing. Up or down, we didn't draw rein till we came to Dan's hotel.

There was the river gleaming before us under a rainbow mist that hallowed every shape. There seemed affinity between the earth and the sky. I've never seen that particular soft unity out of Devon. And every ship, however black or modern, on those pale waters, had the look of a dream ship. The tall green woods, the red earth, the white houses, were all melted into one opal haze. It was raining, but the sun was shining behind. Gulls swooped by us—ghosts of the old greedy wanderers of the sea.

We had told our two boatmen to pull us out to the Pied Witch! They started with great resolution, then rested on their oars.

"The Pied Witch, zurr?" asked one politely; "an' which may her be?"

That's the West countryman all over! Never say you "nay," never lose an opportunity, never own he doesn't know, or can't do anything—independence, amiability, and an eye to the main chance. We mentioned Pearse's name.

"Capt'n Zach'ry Pearse!" They exchanged a look half-amused, half-admiring.

"The Zunflaower, yu mane. That's her. Zunflaower, ahoy!" As we mounted the steamer's black side I heard one say:

"Pied Witch! A pra-aper name that—a dandy name for her!" They laughed as they made fast.

The mate of the Sunflower, or Pied Witch, or whatever she was called, met us—a tall young fellow in his shirtsleeves, tanned to the roots of his hair, with sinewy, tattooed arms, and grey eyes, charred round the rims from staring at weather.

"The skipper is on board," he said. "We're rather busy, as you see. Get on with that, you sea-cooks," he bawled at two fellows who were doing nothing. All over the ship, men were hauling, splicing, and stowing cargo.

"To-day's Friday: we're off on Wednesday with any luck. Will you come this way?" He led us down the companion to a dark hole which he called the saloon. "Names? What! are you Mr. Treffry? Then we're partners!" A schoolboy's glee came on his face.

"Look here!" he said; "I can show you something," and he unlocked the door of a cabin. There appeared to be nothing in it but a huge piece of tarpaulin, which depended, bulging, from the topmost bunk. He pulled it up. The lower bunk had been removed, and in its place was the ugly body of a dismounted Gatling gun.

"Got six of them," he whispered, with unholy mystery, through which his native frankness gaped out. "Worth their weight in gold out there just now, the skipper says. Got a heap of rifles, too, and lots of ammunition. He's given me a share. This is better than the P. and O., and playing deck cricket with the passengers. I'd made up my mind already to chuck that, and go in for plantin' sugar, when I ran across the skipper. Wonderful chap, the skipper! I'll go and tell him. He's been out all night; only came aboard at four bells; having a nap now, but he won't mind that for you."

Off he went. I wondered what there was in Zachary Pearse to attract a youngster of this sort; one of the customary twelve children of some country parson, no doubt-burning to shoot a few niggers, and for ever frank and youthful.

He came back with his hands full of bottles.

"What'll you drink? The skipper'll be here in a jiffy. Excuse my goin' on deck. We're so busy."

And in five minutes Zachary Pearse did come. He made no attempt to shake hands, for which I respected him. His face looked worn, and more defiant than usual.

"Well, gentlemen?" he said.

"We've come to ask what you're going to do?" said Dan.

"I don't know," answered Pearse, "that that's any of your business."

Dan's little eyes were like the eyes of an angry pig.

"You've got five hundred pounds of mine," he said; "why do you think I gave it you?"

Zachary bit his fingers.

"That's no concern of mine," he said. "I sail on Wednesday. Your money's safe."

"Do you know what I think of you?" said Dan.

"No, and you'd better not tell me!" Then, with one of his peculiar changes, he smiled: "As you like, though."

Dan's face grew very dark. "Give me a plain answer," he said: "What are you going to do about her?"

Zachary looked up at him from under his brows.

"Nothing."

"Are you cur enough to deny that you've married her?"

Zachary looked at him coolly. "Not at all," he said.

"What in God's name did you do it for?"

"You've no monopoly in the post of husband, Mr. Treffry."

"To put a child in that position! Haven't you the heart of a man? What d' ye come sneaking in at night for? By Gad! Don't you know you've done a beastly thing?"

Zachary's face darkened, he clenched his fists. Then he seemed to shut his anger into himself.

"You wanted me to leave her to you," he sneered. "I gave her my promise that I'd take her out there, and we'd have gone off on Wednesday quietly enough, if you hadn't come and nosed the whole thing out with your infernal dog. The fat's in the fire! There's no reason why I should take her now. I'll come back to her a rich man, or not at all."

"And in the meantime?" I slipped in.

He turned to me, in an ingratiating way.

"I would have taken her to save the fuss—I really would—it's not my fault the thing's come out. I'm on a risky job. To have her with me might ruin the whole thing; it would affect my nerve. It isn't safe for her."

"And what's her position to be," I said, "while you're away? Do you think she'd have married you if she'd known you were going to leave her like this? You ought to give up this business.

"You stole her. Her life's in your hands; she's only a child!"

A quiver passed over his face; it showed that he was suffering.

"Give it up!" I urged.

"My last farthing's in it," he sighed; "the chance of a lifetime."

He looked at me doubtfully, appealingly, as if for the first time in his life he had been given a glimpse of that dilemma of consequences which his nature never recognises. I thought he was going to give in. Suddenly, to my horror, Dan growled, "Play the man!"

Pearse turned his head. "I don't want your advice anyway," he said; "I'll not be dictated to."

"To your last day," said Dan, "you shall answer to me for the way you treat her."

Zachary smiled.

"Do you see that fly?" he said. "Wel—I care for you as little as this," and he flicked the fly off his white trousers. "Good-morning...!"

The noble mariners who manned our boat pulled lustily for the shore, but we had hardly shoved off' when a storm of rain burst over the ship, and she seemed to vanish, leaving a picture on my eyes of the mate waving his cap above the rail, with his tanned young face bent down at us, smiling, keen, and friendly.

.... We reached the shore drenched, angry with ourselves, and with each other; I started sulkily for home.

As I rode past an orchard, an apple, loosened by the rainstorm, came down with a thud.

"The apples were ripe and ready to fall, Oh! heigh-ho! and ready to fall."

I made up my mind to pack, and go away. But there's a strangeness, a sort of haunting fascination in it all. To you, who don't know the people, it may only seem a piece of rather sordid folly. But it isn't the good, the obvious, the useful that puts a spell on us in life. It's the bizarre, the dimly seen, the mysterious for good or evil.

The sun was out again when I rode up to the farm; its yellow thatch shone through the trees as if sheltering a store of gladness and good news. John Ford himself opened the door to me.

He began with an apology, which made me feel more than ever an intruder; then he said:

"I have not spoken to my granddaughter—I waited to see Dan Treffry."

He was stern and sad-eyed, like a man with a great weight of grief on his shoulders. He looked as if he had not slept; his dress was out of order, he had not taken his clothes off, I think. He isn't a man whom you can pity. I felt I had taken a liberty in knowing of the matter at all. When I told him where we had been, he said:

"It was good of you to take this trouble. That you should have had to! But since such things have come to pass—" He made a gesture full of horror. He gave one the impression of a man whose pride was struggling against a mortal hurt. Presently he asked:

"You saw him, you say? He admitted this marriage? Did he give an explanation?"

I tried to make Pearse's point of view clear. Before this old man, with his inflexible will and sense of duty, I felt as if I held a brief for Zachary, and must try to do him justice.

"Let me understand," he said at last. "He stole her, you say, to make sure; and deserts her within a fortnight."

"He says he meant to take her—"

"Do you believe that?"

Before I could answer, I saw Pasiance standing at the window. How long she had been there I don't know.

"Is it true that he is going to leave me behind?" she cried out.

I could only nod.

"Did you hear him your own self?"

"Yes."

She stamped her foot.

"But he promised! He promised!"

John Ford went towards her.

"Don't touch me, grandfather! I hate every one! Let him do what he likes, I don't care."

John Ford's face turned quite grey.

"Pasiance," he said, "did you want to leave me so much?"

She looked straight at us, and said sharply:

"What's the good of telling stories. I can't help its hurting you."

"What did you think you would find away from here?"

She laughed.

"Find? I don't know—nothing; I wouldn't be stifled anyway. Now I suppose you'll shut me up because I'm a weak girl, not strong like men!"

"Silence!" said John Ford; "I will make him take you."

"You shan't!" she cried; "I won't let you. He's free to do as he likes. He's free—I tell you all, everybody—free!"

She ran through the window, and vanished.

John Ford made a movement as if the bottom had dropped out of his world. I left him there.

I went to the kitchen, where Hopgood was sitting at the table, eating bread and cheese. He got up on seeing me, and very kindly brought me some cold bacon and a pint of ale.

"I thart I shude be seeing yu, zurr," he said between his bites; "Therr's no thart to 'atin' 'bout the 'ouse to-day. The old wumman's puzzivantin' over Miss Pasiance. Young girls are skeery critters"—he brushed his sleeve over his broad, hard jaws, and filled a pipe "specially when it's in the blood of 'em. Squire Rick Voisey werr a dandy; an' Mistress Voisey—well, she werr a nice lady tu, but"—rolling the stem of his pipe from corner to corner of his mouth—"she werr a pra-aper vixen."

Hopgood's a good fellow, and I believe as soft as he looks hard, but he's not quite the sort with whom one chooses to talk over a matter like this. I went upstairs, and began to pack, but after a bit dropped it for a book, and somehow or other fell asleep.

I woke, and looked at my watch; it was five o'clock. I had been asleep four hours. A single sunbeam was slanting across from one of my windows to the other, and there was the cool sound of milk dropping into pails; then, all at once, a stir as of alarm, and heavy footsteps.

I opened my door. Hopgood and a coast-guardsman were carrying Pasiance slowly up the stairs. She lay in their arms without moving, her face whiter than her dress, a scratch across the forehead, and two or three drops there of dried blood. Her hands were clasped, and she slowly crooked and stiffened out her fingers. When they turned with her at the stair top, she opened her lips, and gasped, "All right, don't put me down. I can bear it." They passed, and, with a half-smile in her eyes, she said something to me that I couldn't catch; the door was shut, and the excited whispering began again below. I waited for the men to come out, and caught hold of Hopgood. He wiped the sweat off his forehead.

"Poor young thing!" he said. "She fell—down the cliffs—'tis her back—coastguard saw her 'twerr they fetched her in. The Lord 'elp her mebbe she's not broken up much! An' Mister Ford don't know! I'm gwine for the doctor."

There was an hour or more to wait before he came; a young fellow; almost a boy. He looked very grave, when he came out of her room.

"The old woman there fond of her? nurse her well...? Fond as a dog!—good! Don't know—can't tell for certain! Afraid it's the spine, must have another opinion! What a plucky girl! Tell Mr. Ford to have the best man he can get in Torquay—there's C—-. I'll be round the first thing in the morning. Keep her dead quiet. I've left a sleeping draught; she'll have fever tonight."

John Ford came in at last. Poor old man! What it must have cost him not to go to her for fear of the excitement! How many times in the next few hours didn't I hear him come to the bottom of the stairs; his heavy wheezing, and sighing; and the forlorn tread of his feet going back! About eleven, just as I was going to bed, Mrs. Hopgood came to my door.

"Will yu come, sir," she said; "she's asking for yu. Naowt I can zay but what she will see yu; zeems crazy, don't it?" A tear trickled down the old lady's cheek. "Du 'ee come; 'twill du 'err 'arm mebbe, but I dunno—she'll fret else."

I slipped into the room. Lying back on her pillows, she was breathing quickly with half-closed eyes. There was nothing to show that she had wanted me, or even knew that I was there. The wick of the candle, set by the bedside, had been snuffed too short, and gave but a faint light; both window and door stood open, still there was no draught, and the feeble little flame burned quite still, casting a faint yellow stain on the ceiling like the refection from a buttercup held beneath a chin. These ceilings are far too low! Across the wide, squat window the apple branches fell in black stripes which never stirred. It was too dark to see things clearly. At the foot of the bed was a chest, and there Mrs. Hopgood had sat down, moving her lips as if in speech. Mingled with the half-musty smell of age; there were other scents, of mignonette, apples, and some sweet-smelling soap. The floor had no carpet, and there was not one single dark object except the violin, hanging from a nail over the bed. A little, round clock ticked solemnly.

"Why won't you give me that stuff, Mums?" Pasiance said in a faint, sharp voice. "I want to sleep."

"Have you much pain?" I asked.

"Of course I have; it's everywhere."

She turned her face towards me.

"You thought I did it on purpose, but you're wrong. If I had, I'd have done it better than this. I wouldn't have this brutal pain." She put her fingers over her eyes. "It's horrible to complain! Only it's so bad! But I won't again—promise."

She took the sleeping draught gratefully, making a face, like a child after a powder.

"How long do you think it'll be before I can play again? Oh! I forgot—there are other things to think about." She held out her hand to me. "Look at my ring. Married—isn't it funny? Ha, ha! Nobody will ever understand—that's funny too! Poor Gran! You see, there wasn't any reason—only me. That's the only reason I'm telling you now; Mums is there—but she doesn't count; why don't you count, Mums?"

The fever was fighting against the draught; she had tossed the clothes back from her throat, and now and then raised one thin arm a little, as if it eased her; her eyes had grown large, and innocent like a child's; the candle, too, had flared, and was burning clearly.

"Nobody is to tell him—nobody at all; promise...! If I hadn't slipped, it would have been different. What would have happened then? You can't tell; and I can't—that's funny! Do you think I loved him? Nobody marries without love, do they? Not quite without love, I mean. But you see I wanted to be free, he said he'd take me; and now he's left me after all! I won't be left, I can't! When I came to the cliff—that bit where the ivy grows right down—there was just the sea there, underneath; so I thought I would throw myself over and it would be all quiet; and I climbed on a ledge, it looked easier from there, but it was so high, I wanted to get back; and then my foot slipped; and now it's all pain. You can't think much, when you're in pain."

From her eyes I saw that she was dropping off.

"Nobody can take you away from-yourself. He's not to be told—not even—I don't—want you—to go away, because—" But her eyes closed, and she dropped off to sleep.

They don't seem to know this morning whether she is better or worse....

VI - "Tuesday, 9th August.

.... It seems more like three weeks than three days since I wrote. The time passes slowly in a sickhouse...! The doctors were here this morning, they give her forty hours. Not a word of complaint has passed her lips since she knew. To see her you would hardly think her ill; her cheeks have not had time to waste or lose their colour. There is not much pain, but a slow, creeping numbness.... It was John Ford's wish that she should be told. She just turned her head to the wall and sighed; then to poor old Mrs. Hopgood, who was crying her heart out: "Don't cry, Mums, I don't care."

When they had gone, she asked for her violin. She made them hold it for her, and drew the bow across the strings; but the notes that came out were so trembling and uncertain that she dropped the bow and broke into a passion of sobbing. Since then, no complaint or moan of any kind....

But to go back. On Sunday, the day after I wrote, as I was coming from a walk, I met a little boy making mournful sounds on a tin whistle.

"Coom ahn!" he said, "the Miss wahnts t' zee yu."

I went to her room. In the morning she had seemed better, but now looked utterly exhausted. She had a letter in her hand.

"It's this," she said. "I don't seem to understand it. He wants me to do something—but I can't think, and my eyes feel funny. Read it to me, please."

The letter was from Zachary. I read it to her in a low voice, for Mrs. Hopgood was in the room, her eyes always fixed on Pasiance above her knitting. When I'd finished, she made me read it again, and yet again. At first she seemed pleased, almost excited, then came a weary, scornful look, and before I'd finished the third time she was asleep. It was a remarkable letter, that seemed to bring the man right before one's eyes. I slipped it under her fingers on the bed-clothes, and went out. Fancy took me to the cliff where she had fallen. I found the point of rock where the cascade of ivy flows down the cliff; the ledge on which she had climbed was a little to my right—a mad place. It showed plainly what wild emotions must have been driving her! Behind was a half-cut cornfield with a fringe of poppies, and swarms of harvest insects creeping and flying; in the uncut corn a landrail kept up a continual charring. The sky was blue to the very horizon, and the sea wonderful, under that black wild cliff stained here and there with red. Over the dips and hollows of the fields great white clouds hung low down above the land. There are no brassy, east-coast skies here; but always sleepy, soft-shaped clouds, full of subtle stir and change. Passages of Zachary's Pearse's letter kept rising to my lips. After all he's the man that his native place, and life, and blood have made him. It is useless to expect idealists where the air is soft and things good to look on (the idealist grows where he must create beauty or comfort for himself); useless to expect a man of law and order, in one whose fathers have stared at the sea day and night for a thousand years—the sea, full of its promises of unknown things, never quite the same, a slave to its own impulses. Man is an imitative animal....

"Life's hard enough," he wrote, "without tying yourself down. Don't think too hardly of me! Shall I make you happier by taking you into danger? If I succeed you'll be a rich woman; but I shall fail if you're with me. To look at you makes me soft. At sea a man dreams of all the good things on land, he'll dream of the heather, and honey—you're like that; and he'll dream of the apple-trees, and the grass of the orchards—you're like that; sometimes he only lies on his back and wishes—and you're like that, most of all like that...."

When I was reading those words I remember a strange, soft, half-scornful look came over Pasiance's face; and once she said, "But that's all nonsense, isn't it...?"

Then followed a long passage about what he would gain if he succeeded, about all that he was risking, the impossibility of failure, if he kept his wits about him. "It's only a matter of two months or so," he went on; "stay where you are, dear, or go to my Dad. He'll be glad to have you. There's my mother's room. There's no one to say 'No' to your fiddle there; you can play it by the sea; and on dark nights you'll have the stars dancing to you over the water as thick as bees. I've looked at them often, thinking of you...."

Pasiance had whispered to me, "Don't read that bit," and afterwards I left it out.... Then the sensuous side of him shows up: "When I've brought this off, there's the whole world before us. There are places I can take you to. There's one I know, not too warm and not too cold, where you can sit all day in the shade and watch the creepers, and the cocoa-palms, still as still; nothing to do or care about; all the fruits you can think of; no noise but the parrots and the streams, and a splash when a nigger dives into a water-hole. Pasiance, we'll go there! With an eighty-ton craft there's no sea we couldn't know. The world's a fine place for those who go out to take it; there's lots of unknown stuff' in it yet. I'll fill your lap, my pretty, so full of treasures that you shan't know yourself. A man wasn't meant to sit at home...."

Throughout this letter—for all its real passion—one could feel how the man was holding to his purpose—the rather sordid purpose of this venture. He's unconscious of it; for he is in love with her; but he must be furthering his own ends. He is vital—horribly vital! I wonder less now that she should have yielded.

What visions hasn't he dangled before her. There was physical attraction, too—I haven't forgotten the look I saw on her face at Black Mill. But when all's said and done, she married him, because she's Pasiance Voisey, who does things and wants "to get back." And she lies there dying; not he nor any other man will ever take her away. It's pitiful to think of him tingling with passion, writing that letter to this doomed girl in that dark hole of a saloon. "I've wanted money," he wrote, "ever since I was a little chap sitting in the fields among the cows.... I want it for you now, and I mean to have it. I've studied the thing two years; I know what I know...."

"The moment this is in the post I leave for London. There are a hundred things to look after still; I can't trust myself within reach of you again till the anchor's weighed. When I re-christened her the Pied Witch, I thought of you—you witch to me...."

There followed a solemn entreaty to her to be on the path leading to the cove at seven o'clock on Wednesday evening (that is, to-morrow) when he would come ashore and bid her good-bye. It was signed, "Your loving husband, Zachary Pearse...."

I lay at the edge of that cornfield a long time; it was very peaceful. The church bells had begun to ring. The long shadows came stealing out from the sheaves; woodpigeons rose one by one, and flapped off to roost; the western sky was streaked with red, and all the downs and combe bathed in the last sunlight. Perfect harvest weather; but oppressively still, the stillness of suspense....

Life at the farm goes on as usual. We have morning and evening prayers. John Ford reads them fiercely, as though he were on the eve of a revolt against his God. Morning and evening he visits her, comes out wheezing heavily, and goes to his own room; I believe, to pray. Since this morning I haven't dared meet him. He is a strong old man—but this will break him up....

VII - "KINGSWEAR, Saturday, 13th August.

.... It's over—I leave here to-morrow, and go abroad.

A quiet afternoon—not a breath up in the churchyard! I was there quite half an hour before they came. Some red cows had strayed into the adjoining orchard, and were rubbing their heads against the railing. While I stood there an old woman came and drove them away; afterwards, she stooped and picked up the apples that had fallen before their time.

"The apples are ripe and ready to fall, Oh! heigh-ho! and ready to fall; There came an old woman and gathered them all, Oh! heigh-ho! and gathered them all."

.... They brought Pasiance very simply—no hideous funeral trappings, thank God—the farm hands carried her, and there was no one there but John Ford, the Hopgoods, myself, and that young doctor. They read the service over her grave. I can hear John Ford's "Amen!" now. When it was over he walked away bareheaded in the sun, without a word. I went up there again this evening, and wandered amongst the tombstones. "Richard Voisey," "John, the son of Richard and Constance Voisey," "Margery Voisey," so many generations of them in that corner; then "Richard Voisey and Agnes his wife," and next to it that new mound on which a sparrow was strutting and the shadows of the apple-trees already hovering.

I will tell you the little left to tell....

On Wednesday afternoon she asked for me again.

"It's only till seven," she whispered. "He's certain to come then. But if I—were to die first—then tell him—I'm sorry for him. They keep saying: 'Don't talk—don't talk!' Isn't it stupid? As if I should have any other chance! There'll be no more talking after to-night! Make everybody come, please—I want to see them all. When you're dying you're freer than any other time—nobody wants you to do things, nobody cares what you say.... He promised me I should do what I liked if I married him—I never believed that really—but now I can do what I like; and say all the things I want to." She lay back silent; she could not after all speak the inmost thoughts that are in each of us, so sacred that they melt away at the approach of words.

I shall remember her like that—with the gleam of a smile in her half-closed eyes, her red lips parted—such a quaint look of mockery, pleasure, regret, on her little round, upturned face; the room white, and fresh with flowers, the breeze guttering the apple-leaves against the window. In the night they had unhooked the violin and taken it away; she had not missed it.... When Dan came, I gave up my place to him. He took her hand gently in his great paw, without speaking.

"How small my hand looks there," she said, "too small." Dan put it softly back on the bedclothes and wiped his forehead. Pasiance cried in a sharp whisper: "Is it so hot in here? I didn't know." Dan bent down, put his lips to her fingers and left the room.

The afternoon was long, the longest I've ever spent. Sometimes she seemed to sleep, sometimes whispered to herself about her mother, her grandfather, the garden, or her cats—all sorts of inconsequent, trivial, even ludicrous memories seemed to throng her mind—never once, I think, did she speak of Zachary, but, now and then, she asked the time.... Each hour she grew visibly weaker. John Ford sat by her without moving, his heavy breathing was often the only sound; sometimes she rubbed her fingers on his hand, without speaking. It was a summary of their lives together. Once he prayed aloud for her in a hoarse voice; then her pitiful, impatient eyes signed to me.

"Quick," she whispered, "I want him; it's all so—cold."

I went out and ran down the path towards the cove.

Leaning on a gate stood Zachary, an hour before his time; dressed in the same old blue clothes and leather-peaked cap as on the day when I saw him first. He knew nothing of what had happened. But at a quarter of the truth, I'm sure he divined the whole, though he would not admit it to himself. He kept saying, "It can't be. She'll be well in a few days—a sprain! D' you think the sea-voyage.... Is she strong enough to be moved now at once?"

It was painful to see his face, so twisted by the struggle between his instinct and his vitality. The sweat poured down his forehead. He turned round as we walked up the path, and pointed out to sea. There was his steamer. "I could get her on board in no time. Impossible! What is it, then? Spine? Good God! The doctors.... Sometimes they'll do wonders!" It was pitiful to see his efforts to blind himself to the reality.

"It can't be, she's too young. We're walking very slow." I told him she was dying.

For a second I thought he was going to run away. Then he jerked up his head, and rushed on towards the house. At the foot of the staircase he gripped me by the shoulder.

"It's not true!" he said; "she'll get better now I'm here. I'll stay. Let everything go. I'll stay."

"Now's the time," I said, "to show you loved her. Pull yourself together, man!" He shook all over.

"Yes!" was all he answered. We went into her room. It seemed impossible she was going to die; the colour was bright in her cheeks, her lips trembling and pouted as if she had just been kissed, her eyes gleaming, her hair so dark and crisp, her face so young....

Half an hour later I stole to the open door of her room. She was still and white as the sheets of her bed. John Ford stood at the foot; and, bowed to the level of the pillows, his head on his clenched fists, sat Zachary. It was utterly quiet. The guttering of the leaves had ceased. When things have come to a crisis, how little one feels—no fear, no pity, no sorrow, rather the sense, as when a play is over, of anxiety to get away!

Suddenly Zachary rose, brushed past me without seeing, and ran downstairs.

Some hours later I went out on the path leading to the cove. It was pitch-black; the riding light of the Pied Witch was still there, looking no bigger than a firefly. Then from in front I heard sobbing—a man's sobs; no sound is quite so dreadful. Zachary Pearse got up out of the bank not ten paces off.

I had no heart to go after him, and sat down in the hedge. There was something subtly akin to her in the fresh darkness of the young night; the soft bank, the scent of honeysuckle, the touch of the ferns and brambles. Death comes to all of us, and when it's over it's over; but this blind business—of those left behind!

A little later the ship whistled twice; her starboard light gleamed faintly—and that was all....

VIII - "TORQUAY, 30th October.

.... Do you remember the letters I wrote you from Moor Farm nearly three years ago? To-day I rode over there. I stopped at Brixham on the way for lunch, and walked down to the quay. There had been a shower—but the sun was out again, shining on the sea, the brown-red sails, and the rampart of slate roofs.

A trawler was lying there, which had evidently been in a collision. The spiky-bearded, thin-lipped fellow in torn blue jersey and sea-boots who was superintending the repairs, said to me a little proudly:

"Bane in collision, zurr; like to zee over her?" Then suddenly screwing up his little blue eyes, he added:

"Why, I remembers yu. Steered yu along o' the young lady in this yer very craft."

It was Prawle, Zachary Pearse's henchman.

"Yes," he went on, "that's the cutter."

"And Captain Pearse?"

He leant his back against the quay, and spat. "He was a pra-aper man; I never zane none like 'en."

"Did you do any good out there?"

Prawle gave me a sharp glance.

"Gude? No, t'was arrm we done, vrom ztart to finish—had trouble all the time. What a man cude du, the skipper did. When yu caan't du right, zome calls it 'Providence'! 'Tis all my eye an' Betty Martin! What I zay es, 'tis these times, there's such a dale o' folk, a dale of puzzivantin' fellers; the world's to small."

With these words there flashed across me a vision of Drake crushed into our modern life by the shrinkage of the world; Drake caught in the meshes of red tape, electric wires, and all the lofty appliances of our civilization. Does a type survive its age; live on into times that have no room for it? The blood is there—and sometimes there's a throw-back.... All fancy! Eh?

"So," I said, "you failed?"

Prawle wriggled.

"I wudden' goo for to zay that, zurr—'tis an ugly word. Da-am!" he added, staring at his boots, "'twas thru me tu. We were along among the haythen, and I mus' nades goo for to break me leg. The capt'n he wudden' lave me. 'One Devon man,' he says to me, 'don' lave anotherr.' We werr six days where we shuld ha' been tu; when we got back to the ship a cruiser had got her for gun-runnin'."

"And what has become of Captain Pearse?"

Prawle answered, "Zurr, I belave 'e went to China, 'tis onsartin."

"He's not dead?"

Prawle looked at me with a kind of uneasy anger.

"Yu cudden' kell 'en! 'Tis true, mun 'll die zome day. But therr's not a one that'll show better zport than Capt'n Zach'ry Pearse."

I believe that; he will be hard to kill. The vision of him comes up, with his perfect balance, defiant eyes, and sweetish smile; the way the hair of his beard crisped a little, and got blacker on the cheeks; the sort of desperate feeling he gave, that one would never get the better of him, that he would never get the better of himself.

I took leave of Prawle and half a crown. Before I was off the quay I heard him saying to a lady, "Bane in collision, marm! Like to zee over her?"

After lunch I rode on to Moor. The old place looked much the same; but the apple-trees were stripped of fruit, and their leaves beginning to go yellow and fall. One of Pasiance's cats passed me in the orchard hunting a bird, still with a ribbon round its neck. John Ford showed me all his latest improvements, but never by word or sign alluded to the past. He inquired after Dan, back in New Zealand now, without much interest; his stubbly beard and hair have whitened; he has grown very stout, and I noticed that his legs are not well under control; he often stops to lean on his stick. He was very ill last winter; and sometimes, they say, will go straight off to sleep in the middle of a sentence.

I managed to get a few minutes with the Hopgoods. We talked of Pasiance sitting in the kitchen under a row of plates, with that clinging smell of wood-smoke, bacon, and age bringing up memories, as nothing but scents can. The dear old lady's hair, drawn so nicely down her forehead on each side from the centre of her cap, has a few thin silver lines; and her face is a thought more wrinkled. The tears still come into her eyes when she talks of her "lamb."

Of Zachary I heard nothing, but she told me of old Pearse's death.

"Therr they found 'en, zo to spake, dead—in th' sun; but Ha-apgood can tell yu," and Hopgood, ever rolling his pipe, muttered something, and smiled his wooden smile.

He came to see me off from the straw-yard. "'Tis like death to the varrm, zurr," he said, putting all the play of his vast shoulders into the buckling of my girths. "Mister Ford—well! And not one of th' old stock to take it when 'e's garn.... Ah! it werr cruel; my old woman's never been hersel' since. Tell 'ee what 'tis—don't du t' think to much."

I went out of my way to pass the churchyard. There were flowers, quite fresh, chrysanthemums, and asters; above them the white stone, already stained:

"PASIANCE

"WIFE OF ZACHARY PEARSE

"'The Lord hath given, and the Lord hath taken away.'"

The red cows were there too; the sky full of great white clouds, some birds whistling a little mournfully, and in the air the scent of fallen leaves....

May, 1900.

TO MY MOTHER

A KNIGHT

I

At Monte Carlo, in the spring of the year 189-, I used to notice an old fellow in a grey suit and sunburnt straw hat with a black ribbon. Every morning at eleven o'clock, he would come down to the Place, followed by a brindled German boarhound, walk once or twice round it, and seat himself on a bench facing the casino. There he would remain in the sun, with his straw hat tilted forward, his thin legs apart, his brown hands crossed between them, and the dog's nose resting on his knee. After an hour or more he would get up, and, stooping a little from the waist, walk slowly round the Place and return up hill. Just before three, he would come down again in the same clothes and go into the casino, leaving the dog outside.

One afternoon, moved by curiosity, I followed him. He passed through the hall without looking at the gambling-rooms, and went into the concert. It became my habit after that to watch for him. When he sat in the Place I could see him from the window of my room. The chief puzzle to me was the matter of his nationality.

His lean, short face had a skin so burnt that it looked like leather; his jaw was long and prominent, his chin pointed, and he had hollows in his cheeks. There were wrinkles across his forehead; his eyes were brown; and little white moustaches were brushed up from the corners of his lips. The back of his head bulged out above the lines of his lean neck and high, sharp shoulders; his grey hair was cropped quite close. In the Marseilles buffet, on the journey out, I had met an Englishman, almost his counterpart in features—but somehow very different! This old fellow had nothing of the other's alert, autocratic self-sufficiency. He was quiet and undemonstrative, without looking, as it were, insulated against shocks and foreign substances. He was certainly no Frenchman. His eyes, indeed, were brown, but hazel-brown, and gentle—not the red-brown sensual eye of the Frenchman. An American? But was ever an American so passive? A German? His moustache was certainly brushed up, but in a modest, almost pathetic way, not in the least Teutonic. Nothing seemed to fit him. I gave him up, and named him "the Cosmopolitan."

Leaving at the end of April, I forgot him altogether. In the same month, however, of the following year I was again at Monte Carlo, and going one day to the concert found myself seated next this same old fellow. The orchestra was playing Meyerbeer's "Prophete," and my neighbour was asleep, snoring softly. He was dressed in the same grey suit, with the same straw hat (or one exactly like it) on his knees, and his hands crossed above it. Sleep had not disfigured him—his little white moustache was still brushed up, his lips closed; a very good and gentle expression hovered on his face. A curved mark showed on his right temple, the scar of a cut on the side of his neck, and his left hand was covered by an old glove, the little forger of which was empty. He woke up when the march was over and brisked up his moustache.

The next thing on the programme was a little thing by Poise from Le joli Gilles, played by Mons. Corsanego on the violin. Happening to glance at my old neighbour, I saw a tear caught in the hollow of his cheek, and another just leaving the corner of his eye; there was a faint smile on his lips. Then came an interval; and while orchestra and audience were resting, I asked him if he were fond of music. He looked up without distrust, bowed, and answered in a thin, gentle voice: "Certainly. I know nothing about it, play no instrument, could never sing a note; but fond of it! Who would not be?" His English was correct enough, but with an emphasis not quite American nor quite foreign. I ventured to remark that he did not care for Meyerbeer. He smiled.

"Ah!" he said, "I was asleep? Too bad of me. He is a little noisy—I know so little about music. There is Bach, for instance. Would you believe it, he gives me no pleasure? A great misfortune to be no musician!" He shook his head.

I murmured, "Bach is too elevating for you perhaps."

"To me," he answered, "any music I like is elevating. People say some music has a bad effect on them. I never found any music that gave me a bad thought—no—no—quite the opposite; only sometimes, as you see, I go to sleep. But what a lovely instrument the violin!" A faint flush came on his parched cheeks. "The human soul that has left the body. A curious thing, distant bugles at night have given me the same feeling." The orchestra was now coming back, and, folding his hands, my neighbour turned his eyes towards them. When the concert was over we came out together. Waiting at the entrance was his dog.

"You have a beautiful dog!"

"Ah! yes, Freda, mia cara, da su mano!" The dog squatted on her haunches, and lifted her paw in the vague, bored way of big dogs when requested to perform civilities. She was a lovely creature—the purest brindle, without a speck of white, and free from the unbalanced look of most dogs of her breed.

"Basta! basta!" He turned to me apologetically. "We have agreed to speak Italian; in that way I keep up the language; astonishing the number of things that dog will understand!" I was about to take my leave, when he asked if I would walk a little way with him—"If you are free, that is." We went up the street with Freda on the far side of her master.

"Do you never 'play' here?" I asked him.

"Play? No. It must be very interesting; most exciting, but as a matter of fact, I can't afford it. If one has very little, one is too nervous."

He had stopped in front of a small hairdresser's shop. "I live here," he said, raising his hat again. "Au revoir!—unless I can offer you a glass of tea. It's all ready. Come! I've brought you out of your way; give me the pleasure!"

I have never met a man so free from all self-consciousness, and yet so delicate and diffident the combination is a rare one. We went up a steep staircase to a room on the second floor. My companion threw the shutters open, setting all the flies buzzing. The top of a plane-tree was on a level with the window, and all its little brown balls were dancing, quite close, in the wind. As he had promised, an urn was hissing on a table; there was also a small brown teapot, some sugar, slices of lemon, and glasses. A bed, washstand, cupboard, tin trunk, two chairs, and a small rug were all the furniture. Above the bed a sword in a leather sheath was suspended from two nails. The photograph of a girl stood on the closed stove. My host went to the cupboard and produced a bottle, a glass, and a second spoon. When the cork was drawn, the scent of rum escaped into the air. He sniffed at it and dropped a teaspoonful into both glasses.

"This is a trick I learned from the Russians after Plevna; they had my little finger, so I deserved something in exchange." He looked round; his eyes, his whole face, seemed to twinkle. "I assure you it was worth it—makes all the difference. Try!" He poured off the tea.

"Had you a sympathy with the Turks?"

"The weaker side—" He paused abruptly, then added: "But it was not that." Over his face innumerable crow's-feet had suddenly appeared, his eyes twitched; he went on hurriedly, "I had to find something to do just then—it was necessary." He stared into his glass; and it was some time before I ventured to ask if he had seen much fighting.

"Yes," he replied gravely, "nearly twenty years altogether; I was one of Garibaldi's Mille in '60."

"Surely you are not Italian?"

He leaned forward with his hands on his knees. "I was in Genoa at that time learning banking; Garibaldi was a wonderful man! One could not help it." He spoke quite simply. "You might say it was like seeing a little man stand up to a ring of great hulking fellows; I went, just as you would have gone, if you'd been there. I was not long with them—our war began; I had to go back home." He said this as if there had been but one war since the world began. "In '60," he mused, "till '65. Just think of it! The poor country. Why, in my State, South Carolina—I was through it all—nobody could be spared there—we were one to three."

"I suppose you have a love of fighting?"

"H'm!" he said, as if considering the idea for the first time. "Sometimes I fought for a living, and sometimes—because I was obliged; one must try to be a gentleman. But won't you have some more?"

I refused more tea and took my leave, carrying away with me a picture of the old fellow looking down from the top of the steep staircase, one hand pressed to his back, the other twisting up those little white moustaches, and murmuring, "Take care, my dear sir, there's a step there at the corner."

"To be a gentleman!" I repeated in the street, causing an old French lady to drop her parasol, so that for about two minutes we stood bowing and smiling to each other, then separated full of the best feeling.

II

A week later I found myself again seated next him at a concert. In the meantime I had seen him now and then, but only in passing. He seemed depressed. The corners of his lips were tightened, his tanned cheeks had a greyish tinge, his eyes were restless; and, between two numbers of the programme, he murmured, tapping his fingers on his hat, "Do you ever have bad days? Yes? Not pleasant, are they?"

Then something occurred from which all that I have to tell you followed. There came into the concert-hall the heroine of one of those romances, crimes, follies, or irregularities, call it what you will, which had just attracted the "world's" stare. She passed us with her partner, and sat down in a chair a few rows to our right. She kept turning her head round, and at every turn I caught the gleam of her uneasy eyes. Some one behind us said: "The brazen baggage!"

My companion turned full round, and glared at whoever it was who had spoken. The change in him was quite remarkable. His lips were drawn back from his teeth; he frowned; the scar on his temple had reddened.

"Ah!" he said to me. "The hue and cry! Contemptible! How I hate it! But you wouldn't understand—!" he broke off, and slowly regained his usual air of self-obliteration; he even seemed ashamed, and began trying to brush his moustaches higher than ever, as if aware that his heat had robbed them of neatness.

"I'm not myself, when I speak of such matters," he said suddenly; and began reading his programme, holding it upside down. A minute later, however, he said in a peculiar voice: "There are people to be found who object to vivisecting animals; but the vivisection of a woman, who minds that? Will you tell me it's right, that because of some tragedy like this—believe me, it is always a tragedy—we should hunt down a woman? That her fellow-women should make an outcast of her? That we, who are men, should make a prey of her? If I thought that...." Again he broke off, staring very hard in front of him. "It is we who make them what they are; and even if that is not so—why! if I thought there was a woman in the world I could not take my hat off to—I—I—couldn't sleep at night." He got up from his seat, put on his old straw hat with trembling fingers, and, without a glance back, went out, stumbling over the chair-legs.

I sat there, horribly disturbed; the words, "One must try to be a gentleman!" haunting me. When I came out, he was standing by the entrance with one hand on his hip and the other on his dog. In that attitude of waiting he was such a patient figure; the sun glared down and showed the threadbare nature of his clothes and the thinness of his brown hands, with their long forgers and nails yellow from tobacco. Seeing me he came up the steps again, and raised his hat.

"I am glad to have caught you; please forget all that." I asked if he would do me the honour of dining at my hotel.

"Dine?" he repeated with the sort of smile a child gives if you offer him a box of soldiers; "with the greatest pleasure. I seldom dine out, but I think I can muster up a coat. Yes—yes—and at what time shall I come? At half-past seven, and your hotel is—? Good! I shall be there. Freda, mia cara, you will be alone this evening. You do not smoke caporal, I fear. I find it fairly good; though it has too much bite." He walked off with Freda, puffing at his thin roll of caporal.

Once or twice he stopped, as if bewildered or beset by some sudden doubt or memory; and every time he stopped, Freda licked his hand. They disappeared round the corner of the street, and I went to my hotel to see about dinner. On the way I met Jules le Ferrier, and asked him to come too.

"My faith, yes!" he said, with the rosy pessimism characteristic of the French editor. "Man must dine!"

At half-past six we assembled. My "Cosmopolitan" was in an old frock-coat braided round the edges, buttoned high and tight, defining more than ever the sharp lines of his shoulders and the slight kink of his back; he had brought with him, too, a dark-peaked cap of military shape, which he had evidently selected as more fitting to the coat than a straw hat. He smelled slightly of some herb.

We sat down to dinner, and did not rise for two hours. He was a charming guest, praised everything he ate—not with commonplaces, but in words that made you feel it had given him real pleasure. At first, whenever Jules made one of his caustic remarks, he looked quite pained, but suddenly seemed to make up his mind that it was bark, not bite; and then at each of them he would turn to me and say, "Aha! that's good—isn't it?" With every glass of wine he became more gentle and more genial, sitting very upright, and tightly buttoned-in; while the little white wings of his moustache seemed about to leave him for a better world.

In spite of the most leading questions, however, we could not get him to talk about himself, for even Jules, most cynical of men, had recognised that he was a hero of romance. He would answer gently and precisely, and then sit twisting his moustaches, perfectly unconscious that we wanted more. Presently, as the wine went a little to his head, his thin, high voice grew thinner, his cheeks became flushed, his eyes brighter; at the end of dinner he said: "I hope I have not been noisy."

We assured him that he had not been noisy enough. "You're laughing at me," he answered. "Surely I've been talking all the time!"

"Mon Dieu!" said Jules, "we have been looking for some fables of your wars; but nothing—nothing, not enough to feed a frog!"

The old fellow looked troubled.

"To be sure!" he mused. "Let me think! there is that about Colhoun at Gettysburg; and there's the story of Garibaldi and the Miller." He plunged into a tale, not at all about himself, which would have been extremely dull, but for the conviction in his eyes, and the way he stopped and commented. "So you see," he ended, "that's the sort of man Garibaldi was! I could tell you another tale of him." Catching an introspective look in Jules's eye, however, I proposed taking our cigars over to the cafe opposite.

"Delightful!" the old fellow said: "We shall have a band and the fresh air, and clear consciences for our cigars. I cannot like this smoking in a room where there are ladies dining."

He walked out in front of us, smoking with an air of great enjoyment. Jules, glowing above his candid shirt and waistcoat, whispered to me, "Mon cher Georges, how he is good!" then sighed, and added darkly: "The poor man!"

We sat down at a little table. Close by, the branches of a plane-tree rustled faintly; their leaves hung lifeless, speckled like the breasts of birds, or black against the sky; then, caught by the breeze, fluttered suddenly.

The old fellow sat, with head thrown back, a smile on his face, coming now and then out of his enchanted dreams to drink coffee, answer our questions, or hum the tune that the band was playing. The ash of his cigar grew very long. One of those bizarre figures in Oriental garb, who, night after night, offer their doubtful wares at a great price, appeared in the white glare of a lamp, looked with a furtive smile at his face, and glided back, discomfited by its unconsciousness. It was a night for dreams! A faint, half-eastern scent in the air, of black tobacco and spice; few people as yet at the little tables, the waiters leisurely, the band soft! What was he dreaming of, that old fellow, whose cigar-ash grew so long? Of youth, of his battles, of those things that must be done by those who try to be gentlemen; perhaps only of his dinner; anyway of something gilded in vague fashion as the light was gilding the branches of the plane-tree.

Jules pulled my sleeve: "He sleeps." He had smilingly dropped off; the cigar-ash—that feathery tower of his dreams—had broken and fallen on his sleeve. He awoke, and fell to dusting it.

The little tables round us began to fill. One of the bandsmen played a czardas on the czymbal. Two young Frenchmen, talking loudly, sat down at the adjoining table. They were discussing the lady who had been at the concert that afternoon.

"It's a bet," said one of them, "but there's the present man. I take three weeks, that's enough 'elle est declassee; ce n'est que le premier pas—'"

My old friend's cigar fell on the table. "Monsieur," he stammered, "you speak of a lady so, in a public place?"

The young man stared at him. "Who is this person?" he said to his companion.

My guest took up Jules's glove that lay on the table; before either of us could raise a finger, he had swung it in the speaker's face. "Enough!" he said, and, dropping the glove, walked away.

We all jumped to our feet. I left Jules and hurried after him. His face was grim, his eyes those of a creature who has been struck on a raw place. He made a movement of his fingers which said plainly. "Leave me, if you please!"

I went back to the cafe. The two young men had disappeared, so had Jules, but everything else was going on just as before; the bandsman still twanging out his czardas; the waiters serving drinks; the orientals trying to sell their carpets. I paid the bill, sought out the manager, and apologised. He shrugged his shoulders, smiled and said: "An eccentric, your friend, nicht wahr?" Could he tell me where M. Le Ferrier was? He could not. I left to look for Jules; could not find him, and returned to my hotel disgusted. I was sorry for my old guest, but vexed with him too; what business had he to carry his Quixotism to such an unpleasant length? I tried to read. Eleven o'clock struck; the casino disgorged a stream of people; the Place seemed fuller of life than ever; then slowly it grew empty and quite dark. The whim seized me to go out. It was a still night, very warm, very black. On one of the seats a man and woman sat embraced, on another a girl was sobbing, on a third—strange sight—a priest dozed. I became aware of some one at my side; it was my old guest.

"If you are not too tired," he said, "can you give me ten minutes?"

"Certainly; will you come in?"

"No, no; let us go down to the Terrace. I shan't keep you long."

He did not speak again till we reached a seat above the pigeon-shooting grounds; there, in a darkness denser for the string of lights still burning in the town, we sat down.

"I owe you an apology," he said; "first in the afternoon, then again this evening—your guest—your friend's glove! I have behaved as no gentleman should." He was leaning forward with his hands on the handle of a stick. His voice sounded broken and disturbed.

"Oh!" I muttered. "It's nothing!"'

"You are very good," he sighed; "but I feel that I must explain. I consider I owe this to you, but I must tell you I should not have the courage if it were not for another reason. You see I have no friend." He looked at me with an uncertain smile. I bowed, and a minute or two later he began....

III

"You will excuse me if I go back rather far. It was in '74, when I had been ill with Cuban fever. To keep me alive they had put me on board a ship at Santiago, and at the end of the voyage I found myself in London. I had very little money; I knew nobody. I tell you, sir, there are times when it's hard for a fighting man to get anything to do. People would say to me: 'Afraid we've nothing for a man like you in our business.' I tried people of all sorts; but it was true—I had been fighting here and there since '60, I wasn't fit for anything—" He shook his head. "In the South, before the war, they had a saying, I remember, about a dog and a soldier having the same value. But all this has nothing to do with what I have to tell you." He sighed again and went on, moistening his lips: "I was walking along the Strand one day, very disheartened, when I heard my name called. It's a queer thing, that, in a strange street. By the way," he put in with dry ceremony, "you don't know my name, I think: it is Brune—Roger Brune. At first I did not recognise the person who called me. He had just got off an omnibus—a square-shouldered man with heavy moustaches, and round spectacles. But when he shook my hand I knew him at once. He was a man called Dalton, who was taken prisoner at Gettysburg; one of you Englishmen who came to fight with us—a major in the regiment where I was captain. We were comrades during two campaigns. If I had been his brother he couldn't have seemed more pleased to see me. He took me into a bar for the sake of old times. The drink went to my head, and by the time we reached Trafalgar Square I was quite unable to walk. He made me sit down on a bench. I was in fact—drunk. It's disgraceful to be drunk, but there was some excuse. Now I tell you, sir" (all through his story he was always making use of that expression, it seemed to infuse fresh spirit into him, to help his memory in obscure places, to give him the mastery of his emotions; it was like the piece of paper a nervous man holds in his hand to help him through a speech), "there never was a man with a finer soul than my friend Dalton. He was not clever, though he had read much; and sometimes perhaps he was too fond of talking. But he was a gentleman; he listened to me as if I had been a child; he was not ashamed of me—and it takes a gentleman not to be ashamed of a drunken man in the streets of London; God knows what things I said to him while we were sitting there! He took me to his home and put me to bed himself; for I was down again with fever." He stopped, turned slightly from me, and put his hand up to his brow. "Well, then it was, sir, that I first saw her. I am not a poet and I cannot tell you what she seemed to me. I was delirious, but I always knew when she was there. I had dreams of sunshine and cornfields, of dancing waves at sea, young trees—never the same dreams, never anything for long together; and when I had my senses I was afraid to say so for fear she would go away. She'd be in the corner of the room, with her hair hanging about her neck, a bright gold colour; she never worked and never read, but sat and talked to herself in a whisper, or looked at me for a long time together out of her blue eyes, a little frown between them, and her upper lip closed firm on her lower lip, where she had an uneven tooth. When her father came, she'd jump up and hang on to his neck until he groaned, then run away, but presently come stealing back on tiptoe. I used to listen for her footsteps on the stairs, then the knock, the door flung back or opened quietly—you never could tell which; and her voice, with a little lisp, 'Are you better today, Mr. Brune? What funny things you say when you're delirious! Father says you've been in heaps of battles!'"

He got up, paced restlessly to and fro, and sat down again. "I remember every word as if it were yesterday, all the things she said, and did; I've had a long time to think them over, you see. Well, I must tell you, the first morning that I was able to get up, I missed her. Dalton came in her place, and I asked him where she was. 'My dear fellow,' he answered, 'I've sent Eilie away to her old nurse's inn down on the river; she's better there at this time of year.' We looked at each other, and I saw that he had sent her away because he didn't trust me. I was hurt by this. Illness spoils one. He was right, he was quite right, for all he knew about me was that I could fight and had got drunk; but I am very quick-tempered. I made up my mind at once to leave him. But I was too weak—he had to put me to bed again. The very next morning he came and proposed that I should go into partnership with him. He kept a fencing-school and pistol-gallery. It seemed like the finger of God; and perhaps it was— who knows?" He fell into a reverie, and taking out his caporal, rolled himself a cigarette; having lighted it, he went on suddenly: "There, in the room above the school, we used to sit in the evenings, one on each side of the grate. The room was on the second floor, I remember, with two windows, and a view of nothing but the houses opposite. The furniture was covered up with chintz. The things on the bookshelf were never disturbed, they were Eilie's—half-broken cases with butterflies, a dead frog in a bottle, a horse-shoe covered with tinfoil, some shells too, and a cardboard box with three speckled eggs in it, and these words written on the lid: 'Missel-thrush from Lucy's tree—second family, only one blown.'" He smoked fiercely, with puffs that were like sharp sighs.

"Dalton was wrapped up in her. He was never tired of talking to me about her, and I was never tired of hearing. We had a number of pupils; but in the evening when we sat there, smoking—our talk would sooner or later—come round to her. Her bedroom opened out of that sitting—room; he took me in once and showed me a narrow little room the width of a passage, fresh and white, with a photograph of her mother above the bed, and an empty basket for a dog or cat." He broke off with a vexed air, and resumed sternly, as if trying to bind himself to the narration of his more important facts: "She was then fifteen—her mother had been dead twelve years—a beautiful, face, her mother's; it had been her death that sent Dalton to fight with us. Well, sir, one day in August, very hot weather, he proposed a run into the country, and who should meet us on the platform when we arrived but Eilie, in a blue sun-bonnet and frock-flax blue, her favourite colour. I was angry with Dalton for not telling me that we should see her; my clothes were not quite—my hair wanted cutting. It was black then, sir," he added, tracing a pattern in the darkness with his stick. "She had a little donkey-cart; she drove, and, while we walked one on each side, she kept looking at me from under her sunbonnet. I must tell you that she never laughed—her eyes danced, her cheeks would go pink, and her hair shake about on her neck, but she never laughed. Her old nurse, Lucy, a very broad, good woman, had married the proprietor of the inn in the village there. I have never seen anything like that inn: sweethriar up to the roof! And the scent—I am very susceptible to scents!" His head drooped, and the cigarette fell from his hand. A train passing beneath sent up a shower of sparks. He started, and went on: "We had our lunch in the parlour—I remember that room very well, for I spent the happiest days of my life afterwards in that inn.... We went into a meadow after lunch, and my friend Dalton fell asleep. A wonderful thing happened then. Eilie whispered to me, 'Let's have a jolly time.' She took me for the most glorious walk. The river was close by. A lovely stream, your river Thames, so calm and broad; it is like the spirit of your people. I was bewitched; I forgot my friend, I thought of nothing but how to keep her to myself. It was such a day! There are days that are the devil's, but that was truly one of God's. She took me to a little pond under an elm-tree, and we dragged it, we two, an hour, for a kind of tiny red worm to feed some creature that she had. We found them in the mud, and while she was bending over, the curls got in her eyes. If you could have seen her then, I think, sir, you would have said she was like the first sight of spring.... We had tea afterwards, all together, in the long grass under some fruit-trees. If I had the knack of words, there are things that I could say." He bent, as though in deference to those unspoken memories. "Twilight came on while we were sitting there. A wonderful thing is twilight in the country! It became time for us to go. There was an avenue of trees close by—like a church with a window at the end, where golden light came through. I walked up and down it with her. 'Will you come again?' she whispered, and suddenly she lifted up her face to be kissed. I kissed her as if she were a little child. And when we said good-bye, her eyes were looking at me across her father's shoulder, with surprise and sorrow in them. 'Why do you go away?' they seemed to say.... But I must tell you," he went on hurriedly, "of a thing that happened before we had gone a hundred yards. We were smoking our pipes, and I, thinking of her—when out she sprang from the hedge and stood in front of us. Dalton cried out, 'What are you here for again, you mad girl?' She rushed up to him and hugged him; but when she looked at me, her face was quite different—careless, defiant, as one might say—it hurt me. I couldn't understand it, and what one doesn't understand frightens one."

IV

"Time went on. There was no swordsman, or pistol-shot like me in London, they said. We had as many pupils as we liked—it was the only part of my life when I have been able to save money. I had no chance to spend it. We gave lessons all day, and in the evening were too tired to go out. That year I had the misfortune to lose my dear mother. I became a rich man—yes, sir, at that time I must have had not less than six hundred a year.

"It was a long time before I saw Eilie again. She went abroad to Dresden with her father's sister to learn French and German. It was in the autumn of 1875 when she came back to us. She was seventeen then—a beautiful young creature." He paused, as if to gather his forces for description, and went on.

"Tall, as a young tree, with eyes like the sky. I would not say she was perfect, but her imperfections were beautiful to me. What is it makes you love—ah! sir, that is very hidden and mysterious. She had never lost the trick of closing her lips tightly when she remembered her uneven tooth. You may say that was vanity, but in a young girl—and which of us is not vain, eh? 'Old men and maidens, young men and children!'

"As I said, she came back to London to her little room, and in the evenings was always ready with our tea. You mustn't suppose she was housewifely; there is something in me that never admired housewifeliness—a fine quality, no doubt, still—" He sighed.

"No," he resumed, "Eilie was not like that, for she was never quite the same two days together. I told you her eyes were like the sky—that was true of all of her. In one thing, however, at that time, she always seemed the same—in love for her father. For me! I don't know what I should have expected; but my presence seemed to have the effect of making her dumb; I would catch her looking at me with a frown, and then, as if to make up to her own nature—and a more loving nature never came into this world, that I shall maintain to my dying day—she would go to her father and kiss him. When I talked with him she pretended not to notice, but I could see her face grow cold and stubborn. I am not quick; and it was a long time before I understood that she was jealous, she wanted him all to herself. I've often wondered how she could be his daughter, for he was the very soul of justice and a slow man too—and she was as quick as a bird. For a long time after I saw her dislike of me, I refused to believe it—if one does not want to believe a thing there are always reasons why it should not seem true, at least so it is with me, and I suppose with all selfish men.

"I spent evening after evening there, when, if I had not thought only of myself, I should have kept away. But one day I could no longer be blind.

"It was a Sunday in February. I always had an invitation on Sundays to dine with them in the middle of the day. There was no one in the sitting-room; but the door of Eilie's bedroom was open. I heard her voice: 'That man, always that man!' It was enough for me, I went down again without coming in, and walked about all day.

"For three weeks I kept away. To the school of course I came as usual, but not upstairs. I don't know what I told Dalton—it did not signify what you told him, he always had a theory of his own, and was persuaded of its truth—a very single-minded man, sir.

"But now I come to the most wonderful days of my life. It was an early spring that year. I had fallen away already from my resolution, and used to slink up—seldom, it's true—and spend the evening with them as before. One afternoon I came up to the sitting-room; the light was failing—it was warm, and the windows were open. In the air was that feeling which comes to you once a year, in the spring, no matter where you may be, in a crowded street, or alone in a forest; only once—a feeling like—but I cannot describe it.

"Eilie was sitting there. If you don't know, sir, I can't tell you what it means to be near the woman one loves. She was leaning on the windowsill, staring down into the street. It was as though she might be looking out for some one. I stood, hardly breathing. She turned her head, and saw me. Her eyes were strange. They seemed to ask me a question. But I couldn't have spoken for the world. I can't tell you what I felt—I dared not speak, or think, or hope. I have been in nineteen battles—several times in positions of some danger, when the lifting of a finger perhaps meant death; but I have never felt what I was feeling at that moment. I knew something was coming; and I was paralysed with terror lest it should not come!" He drew a long breath.

"The servant came in with a light and broke the spell. All that night I lay awake and thought of how she had looked at me, with the colour coming slowly up in her cheeks—

"It was three days before I plucked up courage to go again; and then I felt her eyes on me at once—she was making a 'cat's cradle' with a bit of string, but I could see them stealing up from her hands to my face. And she went wandering about the room, fingering at everything. When her father called out: 'What's the matter with you, Elie?' she stared at him like a child caught doing wrong. I looked straight at her then, she tried to look at me, but she couldn't; and a minute later she went out of the room. God knows what sort of nonsense I talked—I was too happy.

"Then began our love. I can't tell you of that time. Often and often Dalton said to me: 'What's come to the child? Nothing I can do pleases her.' All the love she had given him was now for me; but he was too simple and straight to see what was going on. How many times haven't I felt criminal towards him! But when you're happy, with the tide in your favour, you become a coward at once...."

V

"Well, sir," he went on, "we were married on her eighteenth birthday. It was a long time before Dalton became aware of our love. But one day he said to me with a very grave look:

"'Eilie has told me, Brune; I forbid it. She's too young, and you're—too old!' I was then forty-five, my hair as black and thick as a rook's feathers, and I was strong and active. I answered him: 'We shall be married within a month!' We parted in anger. It was a May night, and I walked out far into the country. There's no remedy for anger, or, indeed, for anything, so fine as walking. Once I stopped—it was on a common, without a house or light, and the stars shining like jewels. I was hot from walking, I could feel the blood boiling in my veins—I said to myself 'Old, are you?' And I laughed like a fool. It was the thought of losing her—I wished to believe myself angry, but really I was afraid; fear and anger in me are very much the same. A friend of mine, a bit of a poet, sir, once called them 'the two black wings of self.' And so they are, so they are...! The next morning I went to Dalton again, and somehow I made him yield. I'm not a philosopher, but it has often seemed to me that no benefit can come to us in this life without an equal loss somewhere, but does that stop us? No, sir, not often....

"We were married on the 30th of June 1876, in the parish church. The only people present were Dalton, Lucy, and Lucy's husband—a big, red-faced fellow, with blue eyes and a golden beard parted in two. It had been arranged that we should spend the honeymoon down at their inn on the river. My wife, Dalton and I, went to a restaurant for lunch. She was dressed in grey, the colour of a pigeon's feathers." He paused, leaning forward over the crutch handle of his stick; trying to conjure up, no doubt, that long-ago image of his young bride in her dress "the colour of a pigeon's feathers," with her blue eyes and yellow hair, the little frown between her brows, the firmly shut red lips, opening to speak the words, "For better, for worse, for richer, for poorer, in sickness and in health."

"At that time, sir," he went on suddenly, "I was a bit of a dandy. I wore, I remember, a blue frock-coat, with white trousers, and a grey top hat. Even now I should always prefer to be well dressed....

"We had an excellent lunch, and drank Veuve Clicquot, a wine that you cannot get in these days! Dalton came with us to the railway station. I can't bear partings; and yet, they must come.

"That evening we walked out in the cool under the aspen-trees. What should I remember in all my life if not that night—the young bullocks snuffling in the gateways—the campion flowers all lighted up along the hedges—the moon with a halo-bats, too, in and out among the stems, and the shadows of the cottages as black and soft as that sea down there. For a long time we stood on the river-bank beneath a lime-tree. The scent of the lime flowers! A man can only endure about half his joy; about half his sorrow. Lucy and her husband," he went on, presently, "his name was Frank Tor—a man like an old Viking, who ate nothing but milk, bread, and fruit—were very good to us! It was like Paradise in that inn—though the commissariat, I am bound to say, was limited. The sweethriar grew round our bedroom windows; when the breeze blew the leaves across the opening—it was like a bath of perfume. Eilie grew as brown as a gipsy while we were there. I don't think any man could have loved her more than I did. But there were times when my heart stood still; it didn't seem as if she understood how much I loved her. One day, I remember, she coaxed me to take her camping. We drifted down-stream all the afternoon, and in the evening pulled into the reeds under the willow-boughs and lit a fire for her to cook by—though, as a matter of fact, our provisions were cooked already—but you know how it is; all the romance was in having a real fire. 'We won't pretend,' she kept saying. While we were eating our supper a hare came to our clearing—a big fellow—how surprised he looked! 'The tall hare,' Eilie called him. After that we sat by the ashes and watched the shadows, till at last she roamed away from me. The time went very slowly; I got up to look for her. It was past sundown. I called and called. It was a long time before I found her—and she was like a wild thing, hot and flushed, her pretty frock torn, her hands and face scratched, her hair down, like some beautiful creature of the woods. If one loves, a little thing will scare one. I didn't think she had noticed my fright; but when we got back to the boat she threw her arms round my neck, and said, 'I won't ever leave you again!'

"Once in the night I woke—a water-hen was crying, and in the moonlight a kingfisher flew across. The wonder on the river—the wonder of the moon and trees, the soft bright mist, the stillness! It was like another world, peaceful, enchanted, far holier than ours. It seemed like a vision of the thoughts that come to one—how seldom! and go if one tries to grasp them. Magic—poetry-sacred!" He was silent a minute, then went on in a wistful voice: "I looked at her, sleeping like a child, with her hair loose, and her lips apart, and I thought: 'God do so to me, if ever I bring her pain!' How was I to understand her? the mystery and innocence of her soul! The river has had all my light and all my darkness, the happiest days, and the hours when I've despaired; and I like to think of it, for, you know, in time bitter memories fade, only the good remain.... Yet the good have their own pain, a different kind of aching, for we shall never get them back. Sir," he said, turning to me with a faint smile, "it's no use crying over spilt milk.... In the neighbourhood of Lucy's inn, the Rose and Maybush—Can you imagine a prettier name? I have been all over the world, and nowhere found names so pretty as in the English country. There, too, every blade of grass; and flower, has a kind of pride about it; knows it will be cared for; and all the roads, trees, and cottages, seem to be certain that they will live for ever.... But I was going to tell you: Half a mile from the inn was a quiet old house which we used to call the 'Convent'—though I believe it was a farm. We spent many afternoons there, trespassing in the orchard—Eilie was fond of trespassing; if there were a long way round across somebody else's property, she would always take it. We spent our last afternoon in that orchard, lying in the long grass. I was reading Childe Harold for the first time—a wonderful, a memorable poem! I was at that passage—the bull-fight—you remember:

  "'Thrice sounds the clarion; lo! the signal falls,

    The din expands, and expectation mute'

—"when suddenly Eilie said: 'Suppose I were to leave off loving you?' It was as if some one had struck me in the face. I jumped up, and tried to take her in my arms, but she slipped away; then she turned, and began laughing softly. I laughed too. I don't know why...."

VI

"We went back to London the next day; we lived quite close to the school, and about five days a week Dalton came to dine with us. He would have come every day, if he had not been the sort of man who refuses to consult his own pleasure. We had more pupils than ever. In my leisure I taught my wife to fence. I have never seen any one so lithe and quick; or so beautiful as she looked in her fencing dress, with embroidered shoes.

"I was completely happy. When a man has obtained his desire he becomes careless and self-satisfied; I was watchful, however, for I knew that I was naturally a selfish man. I studied to arrange my time and save my money, to give her as much pleasure as I could. What she loved best in the world just then was riding. I bought a horse for her, and in the evenings of the spring and summer we rode together; but when it was too dark to go out late, she would ride alone, great distances, sometimes spend the whole day in the saddle, and come back so tired she could hardly walk upstairs—I can't say that I liked that. It made me nervous, she was so headlong—but I didn't think it right to interfere with her. I had a good deal of anxiety about money, for though I worked hard and made more than ever, there never seemed enough. I was anxious to save—I hoped, of course—but we had no child, and this was a trouble to me. She grew more beautiful than ever, and I think was happy. Has it ever struck you that each one of us lives on the edge of a volcano? There is, I imagine, no one who has not some affection or interest so strong that he counts the rest for nothing, beside it. No doubt a man may live his life through without discovering that. But some of us—! I am not complaining; what is—is." He pulled the cap lower over his eyes, and clutched his hands firmly on the top of his stick. He was like a man who rushes his horse at some hopeless fence, unwilling to give himself time, for fear of craning at the last moment. "In the spring of '78, a new pupil came to me, a young man of twenty-one who was destined for the army. I took a fancy to him, and did my best to turn him into a good swordsman; but there was a kind of perverse recklessness in him; for a few minutes one would make a great impression, then he would grow utterly careless. 'Francis,' I would say, 'if I were you I should be ashamed.' 'Mr. Brune,' he would answer, 'why should I be ashamed? I didn't make myself.' God knows, I wish to do him justice, he had a heart—one day he drove up in a cab, and brought in his poor dog, who had been run over, and was dying: For half an hour he shut himself up with its body, we could hear him sobbing like a child; he came out with his eyes all red, and cried: 'I know where to find the brute who drove over him,' and off he rushed. He had beautiful Italian eyes; a slight figure, not very tall; dark hair, a little dark moustache; and his lips were always a trifle parted—it was that, and his walk, and the way he drooped his eyelids, which gave him a peculiar, soft, proud look. I used to tell him that he'd never make a soldier! 'Oh!' he'd answer, 'that'll be all right when the time comes! He believed in a kind of luck that was to do everything for him, when the time came. One day he came in as I was giving Eilie her lesson. This was the first time they saw each other. After that he came more often, and sometimes stayed to dinner with us. I won't deny, sir, that I was glad to welcome him; I thought it good for Eilie. Can there be anything more odious," he burst out, "than such a self-complacent blindness? There are people who say, 'Poor man, he had such faith!' Faith, sir! Conceit! I was a fool—in this world one pays for folly....

"The summer came; and one Saturday in early June, Eilie, I, and Francis—I won't tell you his other name—went riding. The night had been wet; there was no dust, and presently the sun came out—a glorious day! We rode a long way. About seven o'clock we started back-slowly, for it was still hot, and there was all the cool of night before us. It was nine o'clock when we came to Richmond Park. A grand place, Richmond Park; and in that half-light wonderful, the deer moving so softly, you might have thought they were spirits. We were silent too—great trees have that effect on me....

"Who can say when changes come? Like a shift of the wind, the old passes, the new is on you. I am telling you now of a change like that. Without a sign of warning, Eilie put her horse into a gallop. 'What are you doing?' I shouted. She looked back with a smile, then he dashed past me too. A hornet might have stung them both: they galloped over fallen trees, under low hanging branches, up hill and down. I had to watch that madness! My horse was not so fast. I rode like a demon; but fell far behind. I am not a man who takes things quietly. When I came up with them at last, I could not speak for rage. They were riding side by side, the reins on the horses' necks, looking in each other's faces. 'You should take care,' I said. 'Care!' she cried; 'life is not all taking care!' My anger left me. I dropped behind, as grooms ride behind their mistresses... Jealousy! No torture is so ceaseless or so black.... In those minutes a hundred things came up in me—a hundred memories, true, untrue, what do I know? My soul was poisoned. I tried to reason with myself. It was absurd to think such things! It was unmanly.... Even if it were true, one should try to be a gentleman! But I found myself laughing; yes, sir, laughing at that word." He spoke faster, as if pouring his heart out not to a live listener, but to the night. "I could not sleep that night. To lie near her with those thoughts in my brain was impossible! I made an excuse, and sat up with some papers. The hardest thing in life is to see a thing coming and be able to do nothing to prevent it. What could I do? Have you noticed how people may become utter strangers without a word? It only needs a thought.... The very next day she said: 'I want to go to Lucy's.' 'Alone?' 'Yes.' I had made up my mind by then that she must do just as she wished. Perhaps I acted wrongly; I do not know what one ought to do in such a case; but before she went I said to her: 'Eilie, what is it?' 'I don't know,' she answered; and I kissed her—that was all.... A month passed; I wrote to her nearly every day, and I had short letters from her, telling me very little of herself. Dalton was a torture to me, for I could not tell him; he had a conviction that she was going to become a mother. 'Ah, Brune!' he said, 'my poor wife was just like that.' Life, sir, is a somewhat ironical affair...! He—I find it hard to speak his name—came to the school two or three times a week. I used to think I saw a change, a purpose growing up through his recklessness; there seemed a violence in him as if he chafed against my blade. I had a kind of joy in feeling I had the mastery, and could toss the iron out of his hand any minute like a straw. I was ashamed, and yet I gloried in it. Jealousy is a low thing, sir—a low, base thing! When he asked me where my wife was, I told him; I was too proud to hide it. Soon after that he came no more to the school.

"One morning, when I could bear it no longer, I wrote, and said I was coming down. I would not force myself on her, but I asked her to meet me in the orchard of the old house we called the Convent. I asked her to be there at four o'clock. It has always been my belief that a man must neither beg anything of a woman, nor force anything from her. Women are generous—they will give you what they can. I sealed my letter, and posted it myself. All the way down I kept on saying to myself, 'She must come—surely she will come!'"

VII

"I was in high spirits, but the next moment trembled like a man with ague. I reached the orchard before my time. She was not there. You know what it is like to wait? I stood still and listened; I went to the point whence I could see farthest; I said to myself, 'A watched pot never boils; if I don't look for her she will come.' I walked up and down with my eyes on the ground. The sickness of it! A hundred times I took out my watch.... Perhaps it was fast, perhaps hers was slow—I can't tell you a thousandth part of my hopes and fears. There was a spring of water, in one corner. I sat beside it, and thought of the last time I had been there—and something seemed to burst in me. It was five o'clock before I lost all hope; there comes a time when you're glad that hope is dead, it means rest. 'That's over,' you say, 'now I can act.' But what was I to do? I lay down with my face to the ground; when one's in trouble, it's the only thing that helps—something to press against and cling to that can't give way. I lay there for two hours, knowing all the time that I should play the coward. At seven o'clock I left the orchard and went towards the inn; I had broken my word, but I felt happy.... I should see her—and, sir, nothing—nothing seemed to matter beside that. Tor was in the garden snipping at his roses. He came up, and I could see that he couldn't look me in the face. 'Where's my wife?' I said. He answered, 'Let's get Lucy.' I ran indoors. Lucy met me with two letters; the first—my own—unopened; and the second, this:

"'I have left you. You were good to me, but now—it is no use.

"EILIE.'"

"She told me that a boy had brought a letter for my wife the day before, from a young gentleman in a boat. When Lucy delivered it she asked, 'Who is he, Miss Eilie? What will Mr. Brune say?' My wife looked at her angrily, but gave her no answer—and all that day she never spoke. In the evening she was gone, leaving this note on the bed.... Lucy cried as if her heart would break. I took her by the shoulders and put her from the room; I couldn't bear the noise. I sat down and tried to think. While I was sitting there Tor came in with a letter. It was written on the notepaper of an inn twelve miles up the river: these were the words.

"'Eilie is mine. I am ready to meet you where you like.'"

He went on with a painful evenness of speech. "When I read those words, I had only one thought—to reach them; I ran down to the river, and chose out the lightest boat. Just as I was starting, Tor came running. 'You dropped this letter, sir,' he said. 'Two pair of arms are better than one.' He came into the boat. I took the sculls and I pulled out into the stream. I pulled like a madman; and that great man, with his bare arms crossed, was like a huge, tawny bull sitting there opposite me. Presently he took my place, and I took the rudder lines. I could see his chest, covered with hair, heaving up and down, it gave me a sort of comfort—it meant that we were getting nearer. Then it grew dark, there was no moon, I could barely see the bank; there's something in the dark which drives one into oneself. People tell you there comes a moment when your nature is decided—'saved' or 'lost' as they call it—for good or evil. That is not true, your self is always with you, and cannot be altered; but, sir, I believe that in a time of agony one finds out what are the things one can do, and what are those one cannot. You get to know yourself, that's all. And so it was with me. Every thought and memory and passion was so clear and strong! I wanted to kill him. I wanted to kill myself. But her—no! We are taught that we possess our wives, body and soul, we are brought up in that faith, we are commanded to believe it—but when I was face to face with it, those words had no meaning; that belief, those commands, they were without meaning to me, they were—vile. Oh yes, I wanted to find comfort in them, I wanted to hold on to them—but I couldn't. You may force a body; how can you force a soul? No, no—cowardly! But I wanted to—I wanted to kill him and force her to come back to me! And then, suddenly, I felt as if I were pressing right on the most secret nerve of my heart. I seemed to see her face, white and quivering, as if I'd stamped my heel on it. They say this world is ruled by force; it may be true—I know I have a weak spot in me.... I couldn't bear it. At last I Jumped to my feet and shouted out, 'Turn the boat round!' Tor looked up at me as if I had gone mad. And I had gone mad. I seized the boat-hook and threatened him; I called him fearful names. 'Sir,' he said, 'I don't take such names from any one!' 'You'll take them from me,' I shouted; 'turn the boat round, you idiot, you hound, you fish!...' I have a terrible temper, a perfect curse to me. He seemed amazed, even frightened; he sat down again suddenly and pulled the boat round. I fell on the seat, and hid my face. I believe the moon came up; there must have been a mist too, for I was cold as death. In this life, sir, we cannot hide our faces—but by degrees the pain of wounds grows less. Some will have it that such blows are mortal; it is not so. Time is merciful.

"In the early morning I went back to London. I had fever on me—and was delirious. I dare say I should have killed myself if I had not been so used to weapons—they and I were too old friends, I suppose—I can't explain. It was a long while before I was up and about. Dalton nursed me through it; his great heavy moustache had grown quite white. We never mentioned her; what was the good? There were things to settle of course, the lawyer—this was unspeakably distasteful to me. I told him it was to be as she wished, but the fellow would come to me, with his—there, I don't want to be unkind. I wished him to say it was my fault, but he said—I remember his smile now—he said, that was impossible, would be seen through, talked of collusion—I don't understand these things, and what's more, I can't bear them, they are—dirty.

"Two years later, when I had come back to London, after the Russo-Turkish war, I received a letter from her. I have it here." He took an old, yellow sheet of paper out of a leathern pockethook, spread it in his fingers, and sat staring at it. For some minutes he did not speak.

"In the autumn of that same year she died in childbirth. He had deserted her. Fortunately for him, he was killed on the Indian frontier, that very year. If she had lived she would have been thirty-two next June; not a great age.... I know I am what they call a crank; doctors will tell you that you can't be cured of a bad illness, and be the same man again. If you are bent, to force yourself straight must leave you weak in another place. I must and will think well of women—everything done, and everything said against them is a stone on her dead body. Could you sit, and listen to it?" As though driven by his own question, he rose, and paced up and down. He came back to the seat at last.

"That, sir, is the reason of my behaviour this afternoon, and again this evening. You have been so kind, I wanted!—wanted to tell you. She had a little daughter—Lucy has her now. My friend Dalton is dead; there would have been no difficulty about money, but, I am sorry to say, that he was swindled—disgracefully. It fell to me to administer his affairs—he never knew it, but he died penniless; he had trusted some wretched fellows—had an idea they would make his fortune. As I very soon found, they had ruined him. It was impossible to let Lucy—such a dear woman—bear that burden. I have tried to make provision; but, you see," he took hold of my sleeve, "I, too, have not been fortunate; in fact, it's difficult to save a great deal out of L 190 a year; but the capital is perfectly safe—and I get L 47, 10s. a quarter, paid on the nail. I have often been tempted to reinvest at a greater rate of interest, but I've never dared. Anyway, there are no debts—I've been obliged to make a rule not to buy what I couldn't pay for on the spot.... Now I am really plaguing you—but I wanted to tell you—in case-anything should happen to me." He seemed to take a sudden scare, stiffened, twisted his moustache, and muttering, "Your great kindness! Shall never forget!" turned hurriedly away.

He vanished; his footsteps, and the tap of his stick grew fainter and fainter. They died out. He was gone. Suddenly I got up and hastened after him. I soon stopped—what was there to say?

VIII

The following day I was obliged to go to Nice, and did not return till midnight. The porter told me that Jules le Ferrier had been to see me. The next morning, while I was still in bed, the door was opened, and Jules appeared. His face was very pale; and the moment he stood still drops of perspiration began coursing down his cheeks.

"Georges!" he said, "he is dead. There, there! How stupid you look! My man is packing. I have half an hour before the train; my evidence shall come from Italy. I have done my part, the rest is for you. Why did you have that dinner? The Don Quixote! The idiot! The poor man! Don't move! Have you a cigar? Listen! When you followed him, I followed the other two. My infernal curiosity! Can you conceive a greater folly? How fast they walked, those two! feeling their cheeks, as if he had struck them both, you know; it was funny. They soon saw me, for their eyes were all round about their heads; they had the mark of a glove on their cheeks." The colour began to come back, into Jules's face; he gesticulated with his cigar and became more and more dramatic. "They waited for me. 'Tiens!' said one, 'this gentleman was with him. My friend's name is M. Le Baron de—-. The man who struck him was an odd-looking person; kindly inform me whether it is possible for my friend to meet him?' Eh!" commented Jules, "he was offensive! Was it for me to give our dignity away? 'Perfectly, monsieur!' I answered. 'In that case,' he said, 'please give me his name and ad dress.... I could not remember his name, and as for the address, I never knew it...! I reflected. 'That,' I said, 'I am unable to do, for special reasons.' 'Aha!' he said, 'reasons that will prevent our fighting him, I suppose? 'On the contrary,' I said. 'I will convey your request to him; I may mention that I have heard he is the best swordsman and pistol-shot in Europe. Good-night!' I wished to give them something to dream of, you understand.... Patience, my dear! Patience! I was, coming to you, but I thought I would let them sleep on it—there was plenty of time! But yesterday morning I came into the Place, and there he was on the bench, with a big dog. I declare to you he blushed like a young girl. 'Sir,' he said, 'I was hoping to meet you; last evening I made a great disturbance. I took an unpardonable liberty'—and he put in my hand an envelope. My friend, what do you suppose it contained—a pair of gloves! Senor Don Punctilioso, hein? He was the devil, this friend of yours; he fascinated me with his gentle eyes and his white moustachettes, his humility, his flames—poor man...! I told him I had been asked to take him a challenge. 'If anything comes of it,' I said, 'make use of me!' 'Is that so?' he said. 'I am most grateful for your kind offer. Let me see—it is so long since I fought a duel. The sooner it's over the better. Could you arrange to-morrow morning? Weapons? Yes; let them choose.' You see, my friend, there was no hanging back here; nous voila en train."

Jules took out his watch. "I have sixteen minutes. It is lucky for you that you were away yesterday, or you would be in my shoes now. I fixed the place, right hand of the road to Roquebrune, just by the railway cutting, and the time—five-thirty of the morning. It was arranged that I should call for him. Disgusting hour; I have not been up so early since I fought Jacques Tirbaut in '85. At five o'clock I found him ready and drinking tea with rum in it—singular man! he made me have some too, brrr! He was shaved, and dressed in that old frock-coat. His great dog jumped into the carriage, but he bade her get out, took her paws on his shoulders, and whispered in her ear some Italian words; a charm, hein! and back she went, the tail between the legs. We drove slowly, so as not to shake his arm. He was more gay than I. All the way he talked to me of you: how kind you were! how good you had been to him! 'You do not speak of yourself!' I said. 'Have you no friends, nothing to say? Sometimes an accident will happen!' 'Oh!' he answered, 'there is no danger; but if by any chance—well, there is a letter in my pocket.' 'And if you should kill him?' I said. 'But I shall not,' he answered slyly: 'do you think I am going to fire at him? No, no; he is too young.' 'But,' I said, 'I—'I am not going to stand that!' 'Yes,' he replied, 'I owe him a shot; but there is no danger—not the least danger.' We had arrived; already they were there. Ah bah! You know the preliminaries, the politeness—this duelling, you know, it is absurd, after all. We placed them at twenty paces. It is not a bad place. There are pine-trees round, and rocks; at that hour it was cool and grey as a church. I handed him the pistol. How can I describe him to you, standing there, smoothing the barrel with his fingers! 'What a beautiful thing a good pistol!' he said. 'Only a fool or a madman throws away his life,' I said. 'Certainly,' he replied, 'certainly; but there is no danger,' and he regarded me, raising his moustachette.

"There they stood then, back to back, with the mouths of their pistols to the sky. 'Un!' I cried, 'deux! tirez!' They turned, I saw the smoke of his shot go straight up like a prayer; his pistol dropped. I ran to him. He looked surprised, put out his hand, and fell into my arms. He was dead. Those fools came running up. 'What is it?' cried one. I made him a bow. 'As you see,' I said; 'you have made a pretty shot. My friend fired in the air. Messieurs, you had better breakfast in Italy.' We carried him to the carriage, and covered him with a rug; the others drove for the frontier. I brought him to his room. Here is his letter." Jules stopped; tears were running down his face. "He is dead; I have closed his eyes. Look here, you know, we are all of us cads—it is the rule; but this—this, perhaps, was the exception." And without another word he rushed away....

Outside the old fellow's lodging a dismounted cocher was standing disconsolate in the sun. "How was I to know they were going to fight a duel?" he burst out on seeing me. "He had white hair—I call you to witness he had white hair. This is bad for me: they will ravish my licence. Aha! you will see— this is bad for me!" I gave him the slip and found my way upstairs. The old fellow was alone, lying on the bed, his feet covered with a rug as if he might feel cold; his eyes were closed, but in this sleep of death, he still had that air of faint surprise. At full length, watching the bed intently, Freda lay, as she lay nightly when he was really asleep. The shutters were half open; the room still smelt slightly of rum. I stood for a long time looking at the face: the little white fans of moustache brushed upwards even in death, the hollows in his cheeks, the quiet of his figure; he was like some old knight.... The dog broke the spell. She sat up, and resting her paws on the bed, licked his face. I went downstairs— I couldn't bear to hear her howl. This was his letter to me, written in a pointed handwriting:

"MY DEAR SIR,—Should you read this, I shall be gone. I am ashamed to trouble you—a man should surely manage so as not to give trouble; and yet I believe you will not consider me importunate. If, then, you will pick up the pieces of an old fellow, I ask you to have my sword, the letter enclosed in this, and the photograph that stands on the stove buried with me. My will and the acknowledgments of my property are between the leaves of the Byron in my tin chest; they should go to Lucy Tor— address thereon. Perhaps you will do me the honour to retain for yourself any of my books that may give you pleasure. In the Pilgrim's Progress you will find some excellent recipes for Turkish coffee, Italian and Spanish dishes, and washing wounds. The landlady's daughter speaks Italian, and she would, I know, like to have Freda; the poor dog will miss me. I have read of old Indian warriors taking their horses and dogs with them to the happy hunting-grounds. Freda would come—noble animals are dogs! She eats once a day—a good large meal—and requires much salt. If you have animals of your own, sir, don't forget—all animals require salt. I have no debts, thank God! The money in my pockets would bury me decently—not that there is any danger. And I am ashamed to weary you with details—the least a man can do is not to make a fuss—and yet he must be found ready.—Sir, with profound gratitude, your servant,

"ROGER BRUNE."

Everything was as he had said. The photograph on the stove was that of a young girl of nineteen or twenty, dressed in an old-fashioned style, with hair gathered backward in a knot. The eyes gazed at you with a little frown, the lips were tightly closed; the expression of the face was eager, quick, wilful, and, above all, young.

The tin trunk was scented with dry fragments of some herb, the history of which in that trunk man knoweth not.... There were a few clothes, but very few, all older than those he usually wore. Besides the Byron and Pilgrim's Progress were Scott's Quentin Durward, Captain Marryat's Midshipman Easy, a pocket Testament, and a long and frightfully stiff book on the art of fortifying towns, much thumbed, and bearing date 1863. By far the most interesting thing I found, however, was a diary, kept down to the preceding Christmas. It was a pathetic document, full of calculations of the price of meals; resolutions to be careful over this or that; doubts whether he must not give up smoking; sentences of fear that Freda had not enough to eat. It appeared that he had tried to live on ninety pounds a year, and send the other hundred pounds home to Lucy for the child; in this struggle he was always failing, having to send less than the amount-the entries showed that this was a nightmare to him. The last words, written on Christmas Day, were these "What is the use of writing this, since it records nothing but failure!"

The landlady's daughter and myself were at the funeral. The same afternoon I went into the concert-room, where I had spoken to him first. When I came out Freda was lying at the entrance, looking into the faces of every one that passed, and sniffing idly at their heels. Close by the landlady's daughter hovered, a biscuit in her hand, and a puzzled, sorry look on her face.

September 1900.

TO

MY BROTHER HUBERT GALSWORTHY

SALVATION OF A FORSYTE

I

Swithin Forsyte lay in bed. The corners of his mouth under his white moustache drooped towards his double chin. He panted:

"My doctor says I'm in a bad way, James."

His twin-brother placed his hand behind his ear. "I can't hear you. They tell me I ought to take a cure. There's always a cure wanted for something. Emily had a cure."

Swithin replied: "You mumble so. I hear my man, Adolph. I trained him.... You ought to have an ear-trumpet. You're getting very shaky, James."

There was silence; then James Forsyte, as if galvanised, remarked: "I s'pose you've made your will. I s'pose you've left your money to the family; you've nobody else to leave it to. There was Danson died the other day, and left his money to a hospital."

The hairs of Swithin's white moustache bristled. "My fool of a doctor told me to make my will," he said, "I hate a fellow who tells you to make your will. My appetite's good; I ate a partridge last night. I'm all the better for eating. He told me to leave off champagne! I eat a good breakfast. I'm not eighty. You're the same age, James. You look very shaky."

James Forsyte said: "You ought to have another opinion. Have Blank; he's the first man now. I had him for Emily; cost me two hundred guineas. He sent her to Homburg; that's the first place now. The Prince was there—everybody goes there."

Swithin Forsyte answered: "I don't get any sleep at night, now I can't get out; and I've bought a new carriage—gave a pot of money for it. D' you ever have bronchitis? They tell me champagne's dangerous; it's my belief I couldn't take a better thing."

James Forsyte rose.

"You ought to have another opinion. Emily sent her love; she would have come in, but she had to go to Niagara. Everybody goes there; it's the place now. Rachel goes every morning: she overdoes it—she'll be laid up one of these days. There's a fancy ball there to-night; the Duke gives the prizes."

Swithin Forsyte said angrily: "I can't get things properly cooked here; at the club I get spinach decently done." The bed-clothes jerked at the tremor of his legs.

James Forsyte replied: "You must have done well with Tintos; you must have made a lot of money by them. Your ground-rents must be falling in, too. You must have any amount you don't know what to do with." He mouthed the words, as if his lips were watering.

Swithin Forsyte glared. "Money!" he said; "my doctor's bill's enormous."

James Forsyte stretched out a cold, damp hand "Goodbye! You ought to have another opinion. I can't keep the horses waiting: they're a new pair—stood me in three hundred. You ought to take care of yourself. I shall speak to Blank about you. You ought to have him—everybody says he's the first man. Good-bye!"

Swithin Forsyte continued to stare at the ceiling. He thought: 'A poor thing, James! a selfish beggar! Must be worth a couple of hundred thousand!' He wheezed, meditating on life....

He was ill and lonely. For many years he had been lonely, and for two years ill; but as he had smoked his first cigar, so he would live his life-stoutly, to its predestined end. Every day he was driven to the club; sitting forward on the spring cushions of a single brougham, his hands on his knees, swaying a little, strangely solemn. He ascended the steps into that marble hall—the folds of his chin wedged into the aperture of his collar—walking squarely with a stick. Later he would dine, eating majestically, and savouring his food, behind a bottle of champagne set in an ice-pail—his waistcoat defended by a napkin, his eyes rolling a little or glued in a stare on the waiter. Never did he suffer his head or back to droop, for it was not distinguished so to do.

Because he was old and deaf, he spoke to no one; and no one spoke to him. The club gossip, an Irishman, said to each newcomer: "Old Forsyte! Look at 'um! Must ha' had something in his life to sour 'um!" But Swithin had had nothing in his life to sour him.

For many days now he had lain in bed in a room exuding silver, crimson, and electric light, smelling of opopanax and of cigars. The curtains were drawn, the firelight gleamed; on a table by his bed were a jug of barley-water and the Times. He made an attempt to read, failed, and fell again to thinking. His face with its square chin, looked like a block of pale leather bedded in the pillow. It was lonely! A woman in the room would have made all the difference! Why had he never married? He breathed hard, staring froglike at the ceiling; a memory had come into his mind. It was a long time ago—forty odd years—but it seemed like yesterday....

It happened when he was thirty-eight, for the first and only time in his life travelling on the Continent, with his twin-brother James and a man named Traquair. On the way from Germany to Venice, he had found himself at the Hotel Goldene Alp at Salzburg. It was late August, and weather for the gods: sunshine on the walls and the shadows of the vine-leaves, and at night, the moonlight, and again on the walls the shadows of the vine-leaves. Averse to the suggestions of other people, Swithin had refused to visit the Citadel; he had spent the day alone in the window of his bedroom, smoking a succession of cigars, and disparaging the appearance of the passers-by. After dinner he was driven by boredom into the streets. His chest puffed out like a pigeon's, and with something of a pigeon's cold and inquiring eye, he strutted, annoyed at the frequency of uniforms, which seemed to him both needless and offensive. His spleen rose at this crowd of foreigners, who spoke an unintelligible language, wore hair on their faces, and smoked bad tobacco. 'A queer lot!' he thought. The sound of music from a cafe attracted him; he walked in, vaguely moved by a wish for the distinction of adventure, without the trouble which adventure usually brought with it; spurred too, perhaps, by an after-dinner demon. The cafe was the bier-halle of the 'Fifties, with a door at either end, and lighted by a large wooden lantern. On a small dais three musicians were fiddling. Solitary men, or groups, sat at some dozen tables, and the waiters hurried about replenishing glasses; the air was thick with smoke. Swithin sat down. "Wine!" he said sternly. The astonished waiter brought him wine. Swithin pointed to a beer glass on the table. "Here!" he said, with the same ferocity. The waiter poured out the wine. 'Ah!' thought Swithin, 'they can understand if they like.' A group of officers close by were laughing; Swithin stared at them uneasily. A hollow cough sounded almost in his ear. To his left a man sat reading, with his elbows on the corners of a journal, and his gaunt shoulders raised almost to his eyes. He had a thin, long nose, broadening suddenly at the nostrils; a black-brown beard, spread in a savage fan over his chest; what was visible of the face was the colour of old parchment. A strange, wild, haughty-looking creature! Swithin observed his clothes with some displeasure—they were the clothes of a journalist or strolling actor. And yet he was impressed. This was singular. How could he be impressed by a fellow in such clothes! The man reached out a hand, covered with black hairs, and took up a tumbler that contained a dark-coloured fluid. 'Brandy!' thought Swithin. The crash of a falling chair startled him—his neighbour had risen. He was of immense height, and very thin; his great beard seemed to splash away from his mouth; he was glaring at the group of officers, and speaking. Swithin made out two words: "Hunde! Deutsche Hunde!" 'Hounds! Dutch hounds!' he thought: 'Rather strong!' One of the officers had jumped up, and now drew his sword. The tall man swung his chair up, and brought it down with a thud. Everybody round started up and closed on him. The tall man cried out, "To me, Magyars!"

Swithin grinned. The tall man fighting such odds excited his unwilling admiration; he had a momentary impulse to go to his assistance. 'Only get a broken nose!' he thought, and looked for a safe corner. But at that moment a thrown lemon struck him on the jaw. He jumped out of his chair and rushed at the officers. The Hungarian, swinging his chair, threw him a look of gratitude—Swithin glowed with momentary admiration of himself. A sword blade grazed his—arm; he felt a sudden dislike of the Hungarian. 'This is too much,' he thought, and, catching up a chair, flung it at the wooden lantern. There was a crash—faces and swords vanished. He struck a match, and by the light of it bolted for the door. A second later he was in the street.

II

A voice said in English, "God bless you, brother!"

Swithin looked round, and saw the tall Hungarian holding out his hand. He took it, thinking, 'What a fool I've been!' There was something in the Hungarian's gesture which said, "You are worthy of me!"

It was annoying, but rather impressive. The man seemed even taller than before; there was a cut on his cheek, the blood from which was trickling down his beard. "You English!" he said. "I saw you stone Haynau—I saw you cheer Kossuth. The free blood of your people cries out to us." He looked at Swithin. "You are a big man, you have a big soul—and strong, how you flung them down! Ha!" Swithin had an impulse to take to his heels. "My name," said the Hungarian, "is Boleskey. You are my friend." His English was good.

'Bulsh-kai-ee, Burlsh-kai-ee,' thought Swithin; 'what a devil of a name!' "Mine," he said sulkily, "is Forsyte."

The Hungarian repeated it.

"You've had a nasty jab on the cheek," said Swithin; the sight of the matted beard was making him feel sick. The Hungarian put his fingers to his cheek, brought them away wet, stared at them, then with an indifferent air gathered a wisp of his beard and crammed it against the cut.

"Ugh!" said Swithin. "Here! Take my handkerchief!"

The Hungarian bowed. "Thank you!" he said; "I couldn't think of it! Thank you a thousand times!"

"Take it!" growled Swithin; it seemed to him suddenly of the first importance. He thrust the handkerchief into the Hungarian's hand, and felt a pain in his arm. 'There!' he thought, 'I've strained a muscle.'

The Hungarian kept muttering, regardless of passers-by, "Swine! How you threw them over! Two or three cracked heads, anyway—the cowardly swine!"

"Look here!" said Swithin suddenly; "which is my way to the Goldene Alp?"

The Hungarian replied, "But you are coming with me, for a glass of wine?"

Swithin looked at the ground. 'Not if I know it!' he thought.

"Ah!" said the Hungarian with dignity, "you do not wish for my friendship!"

'Touchy beggar!' thought Swithin. "Of course," he stammered, "if you put it in that way—"

The Hungarian bowed, murmuring, "Forgive me!"

They had not gone a dozen steps before a youth, with a beardless face and hollow cheeks, accosted them. "For the love of Christ, gentlemen," he said, "help me!"

"Are you a German?" asked Boleskey.

"Yes," said the youth.

"Then you may rot!"

"Master, look here!" Tearing open his coat, the youth displayed his skin, and a leather belt drawn tight round it. Again Swithin felt that desire to take to his heels. He was filled with horrid forebodings—a sense of perpending intimacy with things such as no gentleman had dealings with.

The Hungarian crossed himself. "Brother," he said to the youth, "come you in!"

Swithin looked at them askance, and followed. By a dim light they groped their way up some stairs into a large room, into which the moon was shining through a window bulging over the street. A lamp burned low; there was a smell of spirits and tobacco, with a faint, peculiar scent, as of rose leaves. In one corner stood a czymbal, in another a great pile of newspapers. On the wall hung some old-fashioned pistols, and a rosary of yellow beads. Everything was tidily arranged, but dusty. Near an open fireplace was a table with the remains of a meal. The ceiling, floor, and walls were all of dark wood. In spite of the strange disharmony, the room had a sort of refinement. The Hungarian took a bottle out of a cupboard and, filling some glasses, handed one to Swithin. Swithin put it gingerly to his nose. 'You never know your luck! Come!' he thought, tilting it slowly into his mouth. It was thick, too sweet, but of a fine flavour.

"Brothers!" said the Hungarian, refilling, "your healths!"

The youth tossed off his wine. And Swithin this time did the same; he pitied this poor devil of a youth now. "Come round to-morrow!" he said, "I'll give you a shirt or two." When the youth was gone, however, he remembered with relief that he had not given his address.

'Better so,' he reflected. 'A humbug, no doubt.'

"What was that you said to him?" he asked of the Hungarian.

"I said," answered Boleskey, "'You have eaten and drunk; and now you are my enemy!'"

"Quite right!" said Swithin, "quite right! A beggar is every man's enemy."

"You do not understand," the Hungarian replied politely. "While he was a beggar—I, too, have had to beg" (Swithin thought, 'Good God! this is awful!'), "but now that he is no longer hungry, what is he but a German? No Austrian dog soils my floors!"

His nostrils, as it seemed to Swithin, had distended in an unpleasant fashion; and a wholly unnecessary raucousness invaded his voice. "I am an exile—all of my blood are exiles. Those Godless dogs!" Swithin hurriedly assented.

As he spoke, a face peeped in at the door.

"Rozsi!" said the Hungarian. A young girl came in. She was rather short, with a deliciously round figure and a thick plait of hair. She smiled, and showed her even teeth; her little, bright, wide-set grey eyes glanced from one man to the other. Her face was round, too, high in the cheekbones, the colour of wild roses, with brows that had a twist-up at the corners. With a gesture of alarm, she put her hand to her cheek, and called, "Margit!" An older girl appeared, taller, with fine shoulders, large eyes, a pretty mouth, and what Swithin described to himself afterwards as a "pudding" nose. Both girls, with little cooing sounds, began attending to their father's face.

Swithin turned his back to them. His arm pained him.

'This is what comes of interfering,' he thought sulkily; 'I might have had my neck broken!' Suddenly a soft palm was placed in his, two eyes, half-fascinated, half-shy, looked at him; then a voice called, "Rozsi!" the door was slammed, he was alone again with the Hungarian, harassed by a sense of soft disturbance.

"Your daughter's name is Rosy?" he said; "we have it in England—from rose, a flower."

"Rozsi (Rozgi)," the Hungarian replied; "your English is a hard tongue, harder than French, German, or Czechish, harder than Russian, or Roumanian—I know no more."

"What?" said Swithin, "six languages?" Privately he thought, 'He knows how to lie, anyway.'

"If you lived in a country like mine," muttered the Hungarian, "with all men's hands against you! A free people—dying—but not dead!"

Swithin could not imagine what he was talking of. This man's face, with its linen bandage, gloomy eyes, and great black wisps of beard, his fierce mutterings, and hollow cough, were all most unpleasant. He seemed to be suffering from some kind of mental dog-bite. His emotion indeed appeared so indecent, so uncontrolled and open, that its obvious sincerity produced a sort of awe in Swithin. It was like being forced to look into a furnace. Boleskey stopped roaming up and down. "You think it's over?" he said; "I tell you, in the breast of each one of us Magyars there is a hell. What is sweeter than life? What is more sacred than each breath we draw? Ah! my country!" These words were uttered so slowly, with such intense mournfulness, that Swithin's jaw relaxed; he converted the movement to a yawn.

"Tell me," said Boleskey, "what would you do if the French conquered you?"

Swithin smiled. Then suddenly, as though something had hurt him, he grunted, "The 'Froggies'? Let 'em try!"

"Drink!" said Boleskey—"there is nothing like it"; he filled Swithin's glass. "I will tell you my story."

Swithin rose hurriedly. "It's late," he said. "This is good stuff, though; have you much of it?"

"It is the last bottle."

"What?" said Swithin; "and you gave it to a beggar?"

"My name is Boleskey—Stefan," the Hungarian said, raising his head; "of the Komorn Boleskeys." The simplicity of this phrase—as who shall say: What need of further description?—made an impression on Swithin; he stopped to listen. Boleskey's story went on and on. "There were many abuses," boomed his deep voice, "much wrong done—much cowardice. I could see clouds gathering—rolling over our plains. The Austrian wished to strangle the breath of our mouths—to take from us the shadow of our liberty—the shadow—all we had. Two years ago—the year of '48, when every man and boy answered the great voice—brother, a dog's life!—to use a pen when all of your blood are fighting, but it was decreed for me! My son was killed; my brothers taken—and myself was thrown out like a dog—I had written out my heart, I had written out all the blood that was in my body!" He seemed to tower, a gaunt shadow of a man, with gloomy, flickering eyes staring at the wall.

Swithin rose, and stammered, "Much obliged—very interesting." Boleskey made no effort to detain him, but continued staring at the wall. "Good-night!" said Swithin, and stamped heavily downstairs.

III

When at last Swithin reached the Goldene Alp, he found his brother and friend standing uneasily at the door. Traquair, a prematurely dried-up man, with whiskers and a Scotch accent, remarked, "Ye're airly, man!" Swithin growled something unintelligible, and swung up to bed. He discovered a slight cut on his arm. He was in a savage temper—the elements had conspired to show him things he did not want to see; yet now and then a memory of Rozsi, of her soft palm in his, a sense of having been stroked and flattered, came over him. During breakfast next morning his brother and Traquair announced their intention of moving on. James Forsyte, indeed, remarked that it was no place for a "collector," since all the "old" shops were in the hands of Jews or very grasping persons—he had discovered this at once. Swithin pushed his cup aside. "You may do what you like," he said, "I'm staying here."

James Forsyte replied, tumbling over his own words: "Why! what do you want to stay here for? There's nothing for you to do here—there's nothing to see here, unless you go up the Citadel, an' you won't do that."

Swithin growled, "Who says so?" Having gratified his perversity, he felt in a better temper. He had slung his arm in a silk sash, and accounted for it by saying he had slipped. Later he went out and walked on to the bridge. In the brilliant sunshine spires were glistening against the pearly background of the hills; the town had a clean, joyous air. Swithin glanced at the Citadel and thought, 'Looks a strong place! Shouldn't wonder if it were impregnable!' And this for some occult reason gave him pleasure. It occurred to him suddenly to go and look for the Hungarian's house.

About noon, after a hunt of two hours, he was gazing about him blankly, pale with heat, but more obstinate than ever, when a voice above him called, "Mister!" He looked up and saw Rozsi. She was leaning her round chin on her round hand, gazing down at him with her deepset, clever eyes. When Swithin removed his hat, she clapped her hands. Again he had the sense of being admired, caressed. With a careless air, that sat grotesquely on his tall square person, he walked up to the door; both girls stood in the passage. Swithin felt a confused desire to speak in some foreign tongue. "Maam'selles," he began, "er—bong jour-er, your father—pare, comment?"

"We also speak English," said the elder girl; "will you come in, please?"

Swithin swallowed a misgiving, and entered. The room had a worn appearance by daylight, as if it had always been the nest of tragic or vivid lives. He sat down, and his eyes said: "I am a stranger, but don't try to get the better of me, please—that is impossible." The girls looked at him in silence. Rozsi wore a rather short skirt of black stuff, a white shirt, and across her shoulders an embroidered yoke; her sister was dressed in dark green, with a coral necklace; both girls had their hair in plaits. After a minute Rozsi touched the sleeve of his hurt arm.

"It's nothing!" muttered Swithin.

"Father fought with a chair, but you had no chair," she said in a wondering voice.

He doubled the fist of his sound arm and struck a blow at space. To his amazement she began to laugh. Nettled at this, he put his hand beneath the heavy table and lifted it. Rozsi clapped her hands. "Ah! now I see—how strong you are!" She made him a curtsey and whisked round to the window. He found the quick intelligence of her eyes confusing; sometimes they seemed to look beyond him at something invisible—this, too, confused him. From Margit he learned that they had been two years in England, where their father had made his living by teaching languages; they had now been a year in Salzburg.

"We wait," suddenly said. Rozsi; and Margit, with a solemn face, repeated, "We wait."

Swithin's eyes swelled a little with his desire to see what they were waiting for. How queer they were, with their eyes that gazed beyond him! He looked at their figures. 'She would pay for dressing,' he thought, and he tried to imagine Rozsi in a skirt with proper flounces, a thin waist, and hair drawn back over her ears. She would pay for dressing, with that supple figure, fluffy hair, and little hands! And instantly his own hands, face, and clothes disturbed him. He got up, examined the pistols on the wall, and felt resentment at the faded, dusty room. 'Smells like a pot-house!' he thought. He sat down again close to Rozsi.

"Do you love to dance?" she asked; "to dance is to live. First you hear the music—how your feet itch! It is wonderful! You begin slow, quick—quicker; you fly—you know nothing—your feet are in the air. It is wonderful!"

A slow flush had mounted into Swithin's face.

"Ah!" continued Rozsi, her eyes fixed on him, "when I am dancing—out there I see the plains—your feet go one—two—three—quick, quick, quick, quicker—you fly."

She stretched herself, a shiver seemed to pass all down her. "Margit! dance!" and, to Swithin's consternation, the two girls—their hands on each other's shoulders—began shuffling their feet and swaying to and fro. Their heads were thrown back, their eyes half-closed; suddenly the step quickened, they swung to one side, then to the other, and began whirling round in front of him. The sudden fragrance of rose leaves enveloped him. Round they flew again. While they were still dancing, Boleskey came into the room. He caught Swithin by both hands.

"Brother, welcome! Ah! your arm is hurt! I do not forget." His yellow face and deep-set eyes expressed a dignified gratitude. "Let me introduce to you my friend Baron Kasteliz."

Swithin bowed to a man with a small forehead, who had appeared softly, and stood with his gloved hands touching his waist. Swithin conceived a sudden aversion for this catlike man. About Boleskey there was that which made contempt impossible—the sense of comradeship begotten in the fight; the man's height; something lofty and savage in his face; and an obscure instinct that it would not pay to show distaste; but this Kasteliz, with his neat jaw, low brow, and velvety, volcanic look, excited his proper English animosity. "Your friends are mine," murmured Kasteliz. He spoke with suavity, and hissed his s's. A long, vibrating twang quavered through the room. Swithin turned and saw Rozsi sitting at the czymbal; the notes rang under the little hammers in her hands, incessant, metallic, rising and falling with that strange melody. Kasteliz had fixed his glowing eyes on her; Boleskey, nodding his head, was staring at the floor; Margit, with a pale face, stood like a statue.

'What can they see in it?' thought Swithin; 'it's not a tune.' He took up his hat. Rozsi saw him and stopped; her lips had parted with a faintly dismayed expression. His sense of personal injury diminished; he even felt a little sorry for her. She jumped up from her seat and twirled round with a pout. An inspiration seized on Swithin. "Come and dine with me," he said to Boleskey, "to-morrow— the Goldene Alp—bring your friend." He felt the eyes of the whole room on him—the Hungarian's fine eyes; Margit's wide glance; the narrow, hot gaze of Kasteliz; and lastly—Rozsi's. A glow of satisfaction ran down his spine. When he emerged into the street he thought gloomily, 'Now I've done it!' And not for some paces did he look round; then, with a forced smile, turned and removed his hat to the faces at the window.

Notwithstanding this moment of gloom, however, he was in an exalted state all day, and at dinner kept looking at his brother and Traquair enigmatically. 'What do they know of life?' he thought; 'they might be here a year and get no farther.' He made jokes, and pinned the menu to the waiter's coat-tails. "I like this place," he said, "I shall spend three weeks here." James, whose lips were on the point of taking in a plum, looked at him uneasily.

IV

On the day of the dinner Swithin suffered a good deal. He reflected gloomily on Boleskey's clothes. He had fixed an early hour—there would be fewer people to see them. When the time approached he attired himself with a certain neat splendour, and though his arm was still sore, left off the sling....

Nearly three hours afterwards he left the Goldene Alp between his guests. It was sunset, and along the riverbank the houses stood out, unsoftened by the dusk; the streets were full of people hurrying home. Swithin had a hazy vision of empty bottles, of the ground before his feet, and the accessibility of all the world. Dim recollections of the good things he had said, of his brother and Traquair seated in the background eating ordinary meals with inquiring, acid visages, caused perpetual smiles to break out on his face, and he steered himself stubbornly, to prove that he was a better man than either' of his guests. He knew, vaguely, that he was going somewhere with an object; Rozsi's face kept dancing before him, like a promise. Once or twice he gave Kasteliz a glassy stare. Towards Boleskey, on the other hand, he felt quite warm, and recalled with admiration the way he had set his glass down empty, time after time. 'I like to see him take his liquor,' he thought; 'the fellow's a gentleman, after all.' Boleskey strode on, savagely inattentive to everything; and Kasteliz had become more like a cat than ever. It was nearly dark when they reached a narrow street close to the cathedral. They stopped at a door held open by an old woman. The change from the fresh air to a heated corridor, the noise of the door closed behind him, the old woman's anxious glances, sobered Swithin.

"I tell her," said Boleskey, "that I reply for you as for my son."

Swithin was angry. What business had this man to reply for him!

They passed into a large room, crowded with men all women; Swithin noticed that they all looked fit him. He stared at them in turn—they seemed of all classes, some in black coats or silk dresses, others in the clothes of work-people; one man, a cobbler, still wore his leather apron, as if he had rushed there straight from his work. Laying his hand on Swithin's arm, Boleskey evidently began explaining who he was; hands were extended, people beyond reach bowed to him. Swithin acknowledged the greetings with a stiff motion of his head; then seeing other people dropping into seats, he, too, sat down. Some one whispered his name—Margit and Rozsi were just behind him.

"Welcome!" said Margit; but Swithin was looking at Rozsi. Her face was so alive and quivering! 'What's the excitement all about?' he thought. 'How pretty she looks!' She blushed, drew in her hands with a quick tense movement, and gazed again beyond him into the room. 'What is it?' thought Swithin; he had a longing to lean back and kiss her lips. He tried angrily to see what she was seeing in those faces turned all one way.

Boleskey rose to speak. No one moved; not a sound could be heard but the tone of his deep voice. On and on he went, fierce and solemn, and with the rise of his voice, all those faces-fair or swarthy—seemed to be glowing with one and the same feeling. Swithin felt the white heat in those faces—it was not decent! In that whole speech he only understood the one word—"Magyar" which came again and again. He almost dozed off at last. The twang of a czymbal woke him. 'What?' he thought, 'more of that infernal music!' Margit, leaning over him, whispered: "Listen! Racoczy! It is forbidden!" Swithin saw that Rozsi was no longer in her seat; it was she who was striking those forbidden notes. He looked round—everywhere the same unmoving faces, the same entrancement, and fierce stillness. The music sounded muffled, as if it, too, were bursting its heart in silence. Swithin felt within him a touch of panic. Was this a den of tigers? The way these people listened, the ferocity of their stillness, was frightful...! He gripped his chair and broke into a perspiration; was there no chance to get away? 'When it stops,' he thought, 'there'll be a rush!' But there was only a greater silence. It flashed across him that any hostile person coming in then would be torn to pieces. A woman sobbed. The whole thing was beyond words unpleasant. He rose, and edged his way furtively towards the doorway. There was a cry of "Police!" The whole crowd came pressing after him. Swithin would soon have been out, but a little behind he caught sight of Rozsi swept off her feet. Her frightened eyes angered him. 'She doesn't deserve it,' he thought sulkily; 'letting all this loose!' and forced his way back to her. She clung to him, and a fever went stealing through his veins; he butted forward at the crowd, holding her tight. When they were outside he let her go.

"I was afraid," she said.

"Afraid!" muttered Swithin; "I should think so." No longer touching her, he felt his grievance revive.

"But you are so strong," she murmured.

"This is no place for you," growled Swithin, "I'm going to see you home."

"Oh!" cried Rozsi; "but papa and—Margit!"

"That's their look-out!" and he hurried her away.

She slid her hand under his arm; the soft curves of her form brushed him gently, each touch only augmented his ill-humour. He burned with a perverse rage, as if all the passions in him were simmering and ready to boil over; it was as if a poison were trying to work its way out of him, through the layers of his stolid flesh. He maintained a dogged silence; Rozsi, too, said nothing, but when they reached the door, she drew her hand away.

"You are angry!" she said.

"Angry," muttered Swithin; "no! How d'you make that out?" He had a torturing desire to kiss her.

"Yes, you are angry," she repeated; "I wait here for papa and Margit."

Swithin also waited, wedged against the wall. Once or twice, for his sight was sharp, he saw her steal a look at him, a beseeching look, and hardened his heart with a kind of pleasure. After five minutes Boleskey, Margit, and Kasteliz appeared. Seeing Rozsi they broke into exclamations of relief, and Kasteliz, with a glance at Swithin, put his lips to her hand. Rozsi's look said, "Wouldn't you like to do that?" Swithin turned short on his heel, and walked away.

V

All night he hardly slept, suffering from fever, for the first time in his life. Once he jumped out of bed, lighted a candle, and going to the glass, scrutinised himself long and anxiously. After this he fell asleep, but had frightful dreams. His first thought when he woke was, 'My liver's out of order!' and, thrusting his head into cold water, he dressed hastily and went out. He soon left the house behind. Dew covered everything; blackbirds whistled in the bushes; the air was fresh and sweet. He had not been up so early since he was a boy. Why was he walking through a damp wood at this hour of the morning? Something intolerable and unfamiliar must have sent him out. No fellow in his senses would do such a thing! He came to a dead stop, and began unsteadily to walk back. Regaining the hotel, he went to bed again, and dreamed that in some wild country he was living in a room full of insects, where a housemaid—Rozsi—holding a broom, looked at him with mournful eyes. There seemed an unexplained need for immediate departure; he begged her to forward his things; and shake them out carefully before she put them into the trunk. He understood that the charge for sending would be twenty-two shillings, thought it a great deal, and had the horrors of indecision. "No," he muttered, "pack, and take them myself." The housemaid turned suddenly into a lean creature; and he awoke with a sore feeling in his heart.

His eye fell on his wet boots. The whole thing was scaring, and jumping up, he began to throw his clothes into his trunks. It was twelve o'clock before he went down, and found his brother and Traquair still at the table arranging an itinerary; he surprised them by saying that he too was coming; and without further explanation set to work to eat. James had heard that there were salt-mines in the neighbourhood—his proposal was to start, and halt an hour or so on the road for their inspection; he said: "Everybody'll ask you if you've seen the salt-mines: I shouldn't like to say I hadn't seen the salt-mines. What's the good, they'd say, of your going there if you haven't seen the salt-mines?" He wondered, too, if they need fee the second waiter—an idle chap!

A discussion followed; but Swithin ate on glumly, conscious that his mind was set on larger affairs. Suddenly on the far side of the street Rozsi and her sister passed, with little baskets on their arms. He started up, and at that moment Rozsi looked round—her face was the incarnation of enticement, the chin tilted, the lower lip thrust a little forward, her round neck curving back over her shoulder. Swithin muttered, "Make your own arrangements—leave me out!" and hurried from the room, leaving James beside himself with interest and alarm.

When he reached the street, however, the girls had disappeared. He hailed a carriage. "Drive!" he called to the man, with a flourish of his stick, and as soon as the wheels had begun to clatter on the stones he leaned back, looking sharply to right and left. He soon had to give up thought of finding them, but made the coachman turn round and round again. All day he drove about, far into the country, and kept urging the driver to use greater speed. He was in a strange state of hurry and elation. Finally, he dined at a little country inn; and this gave the measure of his disturbance—the dinner was atrocious.

Returning late in the evening he found a note written by Traquair. "Are you in your senses, man?" it asked; "we have no more time to waste idling about here. If you want to rejoin us, come on to

Danielli's Hotel, Venice." Swithin chuckled when he read it, and feeling frightfully tired, went to bed and slept like a log.

VI

Three weeks later he was still in Salzburg, no longer at the Goldene Alp, but in rooms over a shop near the Boleskeys'. He had spent a small fortune in the purchase of flowers. Margit would croon over them, but Rozsi, with a sober "Many tanks!" as if they were her right, would look long at herself in the glass, and pin one into her hair. Swithin ceased to wonder; he ceased to wonder at anything they did. One evening he found Boleskey deep in conversation with a pale, dishevelled-looking person.

"Our friend Mr. Forsyte—Count D....," said Boleskey.

Swithin experienced a faint, unavoidable emotion; but looking at the Count's trousers, he thought: 'Doesn't look much like one!' And with an ironic bow to the silent girls, he turned, and took his hat. But when he had reached the bottom of the dark stairs he heard footsteps. Rozsi came running down, looked out at the door, and put her hands up to her breast as if disappointed; suddenly with a quick glance round she saw him. Swithin caught her arm. She slipped away, and her face seemed to bubble with defiance or laughter; she ran up three steps, stopped, looked at him across her shoulder, and fled on up the stairs. Swithin went out bewildered and annoyed.

'What was she going to say to me?' he kept thinking. During these three weeks he had asked himself all sorts of questions: whether he were being made a fool of; whether she were in love with him; what he was doing there, and sometimes at night, with all his candles burning as if he wanted light, the breeze blowing on him through the window, his cigar, half-smoked, in his hand, he sat, an hour or more, staring at the wall. 'Enough of this!' he thought every morning. Twice he packed fully—once he ordered his travelling carriage, but countermanded it the following day. What definitely he hoped, intended, resolved, he could not have said. He was always thinking of Rozsi, he could not read the riddle in her face—she held him in a vice, notwithstanding that everything about her threatened the very fetishes of his existence. And Boleskey! Whenever he looked at him he thought, 'If he were only clean?' and mechanically fingered his own well-tied cravatte. To talk with the fellow, too, was like being forced to look at things which had no place in the light of day. Freedom, equality, self-sacrifice!

'Why can't he settle down at some business,' he thought, 'instead of all this talk?' Boleskey's sudden diffidences, self-depreciation, fits of despair, irritated him. "Morbid beggar!" he would mutter; "thank God I haven't a thin skin." And proud too! Extraordinary! An impecunious fellow like that! One evening, moreover, Boleskey had returned home drunk. Swithin had hustled him away into his bedroom, helped him to undress, and stayed until he was asleep. 'Too much of a good thing!' he thought, 'before his own daughters, too!' It was after this that he ordered his travelling carriage. The other occasion on which he packed was one evening, when not only Boleskey, but Rozsi herself had picked chicken bones with her fingers.

Often in the mornings he would go to the Mirabell Garden to smoke his cigar; there, in stolid contemplation of the statues—rows of half-heroic men carrying off half-distressful females—he would spend an hour pleasantly, his hat tilted to keep the sun off his nose. The day after Rozsi had fled from him on the stairs, he came there as usual. It was a morning of blue sky and sunlight glowing on the old prim garden, on its yew-trees, and serio-comic statues, and walls covered with apricots and plums. When Swithin approached his usual seat, who should be sitting there but Rozsi—"Good-morning," he stammered; "you knew this was my seat then?"

Rozsi looked at the ground. "Yes," she answered.

Swithin felt bewildered. "Do you know," he said, "you treat me very funnily?"

To his surprise Rozsi put her little soft hand down and touched his; then, without a word, sprang up and rushed away. It took him a minute to recover. There were people present; he did not like to run, but overtook her on the bridge, and slipped her hand beneath his arm.

"You shouldn't have done that," he said; "you shouldn't have run away from me, you know."

Rozsi laughed. Swithin withdrew his arm; a desire to shake her seized him. He walked some way before he said, "Will you have the goodness to tell me what you came to that seat for?"

Rozsi flashed a look at him. "To-morrow is the fete," she answered.

Swithin muttered, "Is that all?"

"If you do not take us, we cannot go."

"Suppose I refuse," he said sullenly, "there are plenty of others."

Rozsi bent her head, scurrying along. "No," she murmured, "if you do not go—I do not wish."

Swithin drew her hand back within his arm. How round and soft it was! He tried to see her face. When she was nearly home he said goodbye, not wishing, for some dark reason, to be seen with her. He watched till she had disappeared; then slowly retraced his steps to the Mirabell Garden. When he came to where she had been sitting, he slowly lighted his cigar, and for a long time after it was smoked out remained there in the silent presence of the statues.

VII

A crowd of people wandered round the booths, and Swithin found himself obliged to give the girls his arms. 'Like a little Cockney clerk!' he thought. His indignation passed unnoticed; they talked, they laughed, each sight and sound in all the hurly-burly seemed to go straight into their hearts. He eyed them ironically—their eager voices, and little coos of sympathy seemed to him vulgar. In the thick of the crowd he slipped his arm out of Margit's, but, just as he thought that he was free, the unwelcome hand slid up again. He tried again, but again Margit reappeared, serene, and full of pleasant humour; and his failure this time appeared to him in a comic light. But when Rozsi leaned across him, the glow of her round cheek, her curving lip, the inscrutable grey gleam of her eyes, sent a thrill of longing through him. He was obliged to stand by while they parleyed with a gipsy, whose matted locks and skinny hands inspired him with a not unwarranted disgust. "Folly!" he muttered, as Rozsi held out her palm. The old woman mumbled, and shot a malignant look at him. Rozsi drew back her hand, and crossed herself. 'Folly!' Swithin thought again; and seizing the girls' arms, he hurried them away.

"What did the old hag say?" he asked.

Rozsi shook her head.

"You don't mean that you believe?"

Her eyes were full of tears. "The gipsies are wise," she murmured.

"Come, what did she tell you?"

This time Rozsi looked hurriedly round, and slipped away into the crowd. After a hunt they found her, and Swithin, who was scared, growled: "You shouldn't do such things—it's not respectable."

On higher ground, in the centre of a clear space, a military band was playing. For the privilege of entering this charmed circle Swithin paid three kronen, choosing naturally the best seats. He ordered wine, too, watching Rozsi out of the corner of his eye as he poured it out. The protecting tenderness of yesterday was all lost in this medley. It was every man for himself, after all! The colour had deepened again in her cheeks, she laughed, pouting her lips. Suddenly she put her glass aside. "Thank you, very much," she said, "it is enough!"

Margit, whose pretty mouth was all smiles, cried, "Lieber Gott! is it not good-life?" It was not a question Swithin could undertake to answer. The band began to play a waltz. "Now they will dance. Lieber Gott! and are the lights not wonderful?" Lamps were flickering beneath the trees like a swarm of fireflies. There was a hum as from a gigantic beehive. Passers-by lifted their faces, then vanished into the crowd; Rozsi stood gazing at them spellbound, as if their very going and coming were a delight.

The space was soon full of whirling couples. Rozsi's head began to beat time. "O Margit!" she whispered.

Swithin's face had assumed a solemn, uneasy expression. A man raising his hat, offered his arm to Margit. She glanced back across her shoulder to reassure Swithin. "It is a friend," she said.

Swithin looked at Rozsi—her eyes were bright, her lips tremulous. He slipped his hand along the table and touched her fingers. Then she flashed a look at him—appeal, reproach, tenderness, all were expressed in it. Was she expecting him to dance? Did she want to mix with the rift-raff there; wish him to make an exhibition of himself in this hurly-burly? A voice said, "Good-evening!" Before them stood Kasteliz, in a dark coat tightly buttoned at the waist.

"You are not dancing, Rozsi Kozsanony?" (Miss Rozsi). "Let me, then, have the pleasure." He held out his arm. Swithin stared in front of him. In the very act of going she gave him a look that said as plain as words: "Will you not?" But for answer he turned his eyes away, and when he looked again she was gone. He paid the score and made his way into the crowd. But as he went she danced by close to him, all flushed and panting. She hung back as if to stop him, and he caught the glistening of tears. Then he lost sight of her again. To be deserted the first minute he was alone with her, and for that jackanapes with the small head and the volcanic glances! It was too much! And suddenly it occurred to him that she was alone with Kasteliz—alone at night, and far from home. 'Well,' he thought, 'what do I care?' and shouldered his way on through the crowd. It served him right for mixing with such people here. He left the fair, but the further he went, the more he nursed his rage, the more heinous seemed her offence, the sharper grew his jealousy. "A beggarly baron!" was his thought.

A figure came alongside—it was Boleskey. One look showed Swithin his condition. Drunk again! This was the last straw!

Unfortunately Boleskey had recognised him. He seemed violently excited. "Where—where are my daughters?" he began.

Swithin brushed past, but Boleskey caught his arm. "Listen—brother!" he said; "news of my country! After to-morrow...."

"Keep it to yourself!" growled Swithin, wrenching his arm free. He went straight to his lodgings, and, lying on the hard sofa of his unlighted sitting-room, gave himself up to bitter thoughts. But in spite of all his anger, Rozsi's supply-moving figure, with its pouting lips, and roguish appealing eyes, still haunted him.

VIII

Next morning there was not a carriage to be had, and Swithin was compelled to put off his departure till the morrow. The day was grey and misty; he wandered about with the strained, inquiring look of a lost dog in his eyes.

Late in the afternoon he went back to his lodgings. In a corner of the sitting-room stood Rozsi. The thrill of triumph, the sense of appeasement, the emotion, that seized on him, crept through to his lips in a faint smile. Rozsi made no sound, her face was hidden by her hands. And this silence of hers weighed on Swithin. She was forcing him to break it. What was behind her hands? His own face was visible! Why didn't she speak? Why was she here? Alone? That was not right surely.

Suddenly Rozsi dropped her hands; her flushed face was quivering—it seemed as though a word, a sign, even, might bring a burst of tears.

He walked over to the window. 'I must give her time!' he thought; then seized by unreasoning terror at this silence, spun round, and caught her by the arms. Rozsi held back from him, swayed forward and buried her face on his breast....

Half an hour later Swithin was pacing up and down his room. The scent of rose leaves had not yet died away. A glove lay on the floor; he picked it up, and for a long time stood weighing it in his hand. All sorts of confused thoughts and feelings haunted him. It was the purest and least selfish moment of his life, this moment after she had yielded. But that pure gratitude at her fiery, simple abnegation did not last; it was followed by a petty sense of triumph, and by uneasiness. He was still weighing the little glove in his hand, when he had another visitor. It was Kasteliz.

"What can I do for you?" Swithin asked ironically.

The Hungarian seemed suffering from excitement. Why had Swithin left his charges the night before? What excuse had he to make? What sort of conduct did he call this?

Swithin, very like a bull-dog at that moment, answered: What business was it of his?

The business of a gentleman! What right had the Englishman to pursue a young girl?

"Pursue?" said Swithin; "you've been spying, then?"

"Spying—I—Kasteliz—Maurus Johann—an insult!"

"Insult!" sneered Swithin; "d'you mean to tell me you weren't in the street just now?"

Kasteliz answered with a hiss, "If you do not leave the city I will make you, with my sword—do you understand?"

"And if you do not leave my room I will throw you out of the window!"

For some minutes Kasteliz spoke in pure Hungarian while Swithin waited, with a forced smile and a fixed look in his eye. He did not understand Hungarian.

"If you are still in the city to-morrow evening," said Kasteliz at last in English, "I will spit you in the street."

Swithin turned to the window and watched his visitor's retiring back with a queer mixture of amusement, stubbornness, and anxiety. 'Well,' he thought, 'I suppose he'll run me through!' The thought was unpleasant; and it kept recurring, but it only served to harden his determination. His head was busy with plans for seeing Rozsi; his blood on fire with the kisses she had given him.

IX

Swithin was long in deciding to go forth next day. He had made up his mind not to go to Rozsi till five o'clock. 'Mustn't make myself too cheap,' he thought. It was a little past that hour when he at last sallied out, and with a beating heart walked towards Boleskey's. He looked up at the window, more than half expecting to see Rozsi there; but she was not, and he noticed with faint surprise that the window was not open; the plants, too, outside, looked singularly arid. He knocked. No one came. He beat a fierce tattoo. At last the door was opened by a man with a reddish beard, and one of those sardonic faces only to be seen on shoemakers of Teutonic origin.

"What do you want, making all this noise?" he asked in German.

Swithin pointed up the stairs. The man grinned, and shook his head.

"I want to go up," said Swithin.

The cobbler shrugged his shoulders, and Swithin rushed upstairs. The rooms were empty. The furniture remained, but all signs of life were gone. One of his own bouquets, faded, stood in a glass; the ashes of a fire were barely cold; little scraps of paper strewed the hearth; already the room smelt musty. He went into the bedrooms, and with a feeling of stupefaction stood staring at the girls' beds, side by side against the wall. A bit of ribbon caught his eye; he picked it up and put it in his pocket—it was a piece of evidence that she had once existed. By the mirror some pins were dropped about; a little powder had been spilled. He looked at his own disquiet face and thought, 'I've been cheated!'

The shoemaker's voice aroused him. "Tausend Teufel! Eilen Sie, nur! Zeit is Geld! Kann nich' Langer warten!" Slowly he descended.

"Where have they gone?" asked Swithin painfully. "A pound for every English word you speak. A pound!" and he made an O with his fingers.

The corners of the shoemaker's lips curled. "Geld! Mf! Eilen Sie, nur!"

But in Swithin a sullen anger had begun to burn. "If you don't tell me," he said, "it'll be the worse for you."

"Sind ein komischer Kerl!" remarked the shoemaker. "Hier ist meine Frau!"

A battered-looking woman came hurrying down the passage, calling out in German, "Don't let him go!"

With a snarling sound the shoemaker turned his back, and shambled off.

The woman furtively thrust a letter into Swithin's hand, and furtively waited.

The letter was from Rozsi.

"Forgive me"—it ran—"that I leave you and do not say goodbye. To-day our father had the call from our dear Father-town so long awaited. In two hours we are ready. I pray to the Virgin to keep you ever safe, and that you do not quite forget me.—Your unforgetting good friend, ROZSI."

When Swithin read it his first sensation was that of a man sinking in a bog; then his obstinacy stiffened. 'I won't be done,' he thought. Taking out a sovereign he tried to make the woman comprehend that she could earn it, by telling him where they had gone. He got her finally to write the words out in his pocket-book, gave her the sovereign, and hurried to the Goldene Alp, where there was a waiter who spoke English. The translation given him was this:

"At three o'clock they start in a carriage on the road to Linz—they have bad horses—the Herr also rides a white horse."

Swithin at once hailed a carriage and started at full gallop on the road to Linz. Outside the Mirabell Garden he caught sight of Kasteliz and grinned at him. 'I've sold him anyway,' he thought; 'for all their talk, they're no good, these foreigners!'

His spirits rose, but soon fell again. What chance had he of catching them? They had three hours' start! Still, the roads were heavy from the rain of the last two nights—they had luggage and bad horses; his own were good, his driver bribed—he might overtake them by ten o'clock! But did he want to? What a fool he had been not to bring his luggage; he would then have had a respectable position. What a brute he would look without a change of shirt, or anything to shave with! He saw himself with horror, all bristly, and in soiled linen. People would think him mad. 'I've given myself away,' flashed across him, 'what the devil can I say to them?' and he stared sullenly at the driver's back. He read Rozsi's letter again; it had a scent of her. And in the growing darkness, jolted by the swinging of the carriage, he suffered tortures from his prudence, tortures from his passion.

It grew colder and dark. He turned the collar of his coat up to his ears. He had visions of Piccadilly. This wild-goose chase appeared suddenly a dangerous, unfathomable business. Lights, fellowship, security! 'Never again!' he brooded; 'why won't they let me alone?' But it was not clear whether by 'they' he meant the conventions, the Boleskeys, his passions, or those haunting memories of Rozsi. If he had only had a bag with him! What was he going to say? What was he going to get by this? He received no answer to these questions. The darkness itself was less obscure than his sensations. From time to time he took out his watch. At each village the driver made inquiries. It was past ten when he stopped the carriage with a jerk. The stars were bright as steel, and by the side of the road a reedy lake showed in the moonlight. Swithin shivered. A man on a horse had halted in the centre of the road. "Drive on!" called Swithin, with a stolid face. It turned out to be Boleskey, who, on a gaunt white horse, looked like some winged creature. He stood where he could bar the progress of the carriage, holding out a pistol.

'Theatrical beggar!' thought Swithin, with a nervous smile. He made no sign of recognition. Slowly Boleskey brought his lean horse up to the carriage. When he saw who was within he showed astonishment and joy.

"You?" he cried, slapping his hand on his attenuated thigh, and leaning over till his beard touched Swithin. "You have come? You followed us?"

"It seems so," Swithin grunted out.

"You throw in your lot with us. Is it possible? You—you are a knight-errant then!"

"Good God!" said Swithin. Boleskey, flogging his dejected steed, cantered forward in the moonlight. He came back, bringing an old cloak, which he insisted on wrapping round Swithin's shoulders. He handed him, too, a capacious flask.

"How cold you look!" he said. "Wonderful! Wonderful! you English!" His grateful eyes never left Swithin for a moment. They had come up to the heels of the other carriage now, but Swithin, hunched in the cloak, did not try to see what was in front of him. To the bottom of his soul he resented the Hungarian's gratitude. He remarked at last, with wasted irony:

"You're in a hurry, it seems!"

"If we had wings," Boleskey answered, "we would use them."

"Wings!" muttered Swithin thickly; "legs are good enough for me."

X

Arrived at the inn where they were to pass the night, Swithin waited, hoping to get into the house without a "scene," but when at last he alighted the girls were in the doorway, and Margit greeted him with an admiring murmur, in which, however, he seemed to detect irony. Rozsi, pale and tremulous, with a half-scared look, gave him her hand, and, quickly withdrawing it, shrank behind her sister. When they had gone up to their room Swithin sought Boleskey. His spirits had risen remarkably. "Tell the landlord to get us supper," he said; "we'll crack a bottle to our luck." He hurried on the landlord's preparations. The window of the room faced a wood, so near that he could almost touch the trees. The scent from the pines blew in on him. He turned away from that scented darkness, and began to draw the corks of winebottles. The sound seemed to conjure up Boleskey. He came in, splashed all over, smelling slightly of stables; soon after, Margit appeared, fresh and serene, but Rozsi did not come.

"Where is your sister?" Swithin said. Rozsi, it seemed, was tired. "It will do her good to eat," said Swithin. And Boleskey, murmuring, "She must drink to our country," went out to summon her, Margit followed him, while Swithin cut up a chicken. They came back without her. She had "a megrim of the spirit."

Swithin's face fell. "Look here!" he said, "I'll go and try. Don't wait for me."

"Yes," answered Boleskey, sinking mournfully into a chair; "try, brother, try-by all means, try."

Swithin walked down the corridor with an odd, sweet, sinking sensation in his chest; and tapped on Rozsi's door. In a minute, she peeped forth, with her hair loose, and wondering eyes.

"Rozsi," he stammered, "what makes you afraid of me, now?"

She stared at him, but did not answer.

"Why won't you come?"

Still she did not speak, but suddenly stretched out to him her bare arm. Swithin pressed his face to it. With a shiver, she whispered above him, "I will come," and gently shut the door.

Swithin stealthily retraced his steps, and paused a minute outside the sitting-room to regain his self-control.

The sight of Boleskey with a bottle in his hand steadied him.

"She is coming," he said. And very soon she did come, her thick hair roughly twisted in a plait.

Swithin sat between the girls; but did not talk, for he was really hungry. Boleskey too was silent, plunged in gloom; Rozsi was dumb; Margit alone chattered.

"You will come to our Father-town? We shall have things to show you. Rozsi, what things we will show him!" Rozsi, with a little appealing movement of her hands, repeated, "What things we will show you!" She seemed suddenly to find her voice, and with glowing cheeks, mouths full, and eyes bright as squirrels', they chattered reminiscences of the "dear Father-town," of "dear friends," of the "dear home."

'A poor place!' Swithin could not help thinking. This enthusiasm seemed to him common; but he was careful to assume a look of interest, feeding on the glances flashed at him from Rozsi's restless eyes.

As the wine waned Boleskey grew more and more gloomy, but now and then a sort of gleaming flicker passed over his face. He rose to his feet at last.

"Let us not forget," he said, "that we go perhaps to ruin, to death; in the face of all this we go, because our country needs—in this there is no credit, neither to me nor to you, my daughters; but for this noble Englishman, what shall we say? Give thanks to God for a great heart. He comes—not for country, not for fame, not for money, but to help the weak and the oppressed. Let us drink, then, to him; let us drink again and again to heroic Forsyte!" In the midst of the dead silence, Swithin caught the look of suppliant mockery in Rozsi's eyes. He glanced at the Hungarian. Was he laughing at him? But Boleskey, after drinking up his wine, had sunk again into his seat; and there suddenly, to the surprise of all, he began to snore. Margit rose and, bending over him like a mother, murmured: "He is tired—it is the ride!" She raised him in her strong arms, and leaning on her shoulder Boleskey staggered from the room. Swithin and Rozsi were left alone. He slid his hand towards her hand that lay so close, on the rough table-cloth. It seemed to await his touch. Something gave way in him, and words came welling up; for the moment he forgot himself, forgot everything but that he was near her. Her head dropped on his shoulder, he breathed the perfume of her hair. "Good-night!" she whispered, and the whisper was like a kiss; yet before he could stop her she was gone. Her footsteps died away in the passage, but Swithin sat gazing intently at a single bright drop of spilt wine quivering on the table's edge. In that moment she, in her helplessness and emotion, was all in all to him—his life nothing; all the real things—his conventions, convictions, training, and himself—all seemed remote, behind a mist of passion and strange chivalry. Carefully with a bit of bread he soaked up the bright drop; and suddenly he thought: 'This is tremendous!' For a long time he stood there in the window, close to the dark pine-trees.

XI

In the early morning he awoke, full of the discomfort of this strange place and the medley of his dreams. Lying, with his nose peeping over the quilt, he was visited by a horrible suspicion. When he could bear it no longer, he started up in bed. What if it were all a plot to get him to marry her? The thought was treacherous, and inspired in him a faint disgust. Still, she might be ignorant of it! But was she so innocent? What innocent girl would have come to his room like that? What innocent girl? Her father, who pretended to be caring only for his country? It was not probable that any man was such a fool; it was all part of the game-a scheming rascal! Kasteliz, too—his threats! They intended him to marry her! And the horrid idea was strengthened by his reverence for marriage. It was the proper, the respectable condition; he was genuinely afraid of this other sort of liaison—it was somehow too primitive! And yet the thought of that marriage made his blood run cold. Considering that she had already yielded, it would be all the more monstrous! With the cold, fatal clearness of the morning light he now for the first time saw his position in its full bearings. And, like a fish pulled out of water, he gasped at what was disclosed. Sullen resentment against this attempt to force him settled deep into his soul.

He seated himself on the bed, holding his head in his hands, solemnly thinking out what such marriage meant. In the first place it meant ridicule, in the next place ridicule, in the last place ridicule. She would eat chicken bones with her fingers—those fingers his lips still burned to kiss. She would dance wildly with other men. She would talk of her "dear Father-town," and all the time her eyes would look beyond him, some where or other into some d—d place he knew nothing of. He sprang up and paced the room, and for a moment thought he would go mad.

They meant him to marry her! Even she—she meant him to marry her! Her tantalising inscrutability; her sudden little tendernesses; her quick laughter; her swift, burning kisses; even the movements of her hands; her tears—all were evidence against her. Not one of these things that Nature made her do counted on her side, but how they fanned his longing, his desire, and distress! He went to the glass and tried to part his hair with his fingers, but being rather fine, it fell into lank streaks. There was no comfort to be got from it. He drew his muddy boots on. Suddenly he thought: 'If I could see her alone, I could arrive at some arrangement!' Then, with a sense of stupefaction, he made the discovery that no arrangement could possibly be made that would not be dangerous, even desperate. He seized his hat, and, like a rabbit that has been fired at, bolted from the room. He plodded along amongst the damp woods with his head down, and resentment and dismay in his heart. But, as the sun rose, and the air grew sweet with pine scent, he slowly regained a sort of equability. After all, she had already yielded; it was not as if...! And the tramp of his own footsteps lulled him into feeling that it would all come right.

'Look at the thing practically,' he thought. The faster he walked the firmer became his conviction that he could still see it through. He took out his watch—it was past seven—he began to hasten back. In the yard of the inn his driver was harnessing the horses; Swithin went up to him.

"Who told you to put them in?" he asked.

The driver answered, "Der Herr."

Swithin turned away. 'In ten minutes,' he thought, 'I shall be in that carriage again, with this going on in my head! Driving away from England, from all I'm used to-driving to-what?' Could he face it? Could he face all that he had been through that morning; face it day after day, night after night? Looking up, he saw Rozsi at her open window gazing down at him; never had she looked sweeter, more roguish. An inexplicable terror seized on him; he ran across the yard and jumped into his carriage. "To Salzburg!" he cried; "drive on!" And rattling out of the yard without a look behind, he flung a sovereign at the hostler. Flying back along the road faster even than he had come, with pale face, and eyes blank and staring like a pug-dog's, Swithin spoke no single word; nor, till he had reached the door of his lodgings, did he suffer the driver to draw rein.

XII

Towards evening, five days later, Swithin, yellow and travel-worn, was ferried in a gondola to Danielli's Hotel. His brother, who was on the steps, looked at him with an apprehensive curiosity.

"Why, it's you!" he mumbled. "So you've got here safe?"

"Safe?" growled Swithin.

James replied, "I thought you wouldn't leave your friends!" Then, with a jerk of suspicion, "You haven't brought your friends?"

"What friends?" growled Swithin.

James changed the subject. "You don't look the thing," he said.

"Really!" muttered Swithin; "what's that to you?"

He appeared at dinner that night, but fell asleep over his coffee. Neither Traquair nor James asked him any further question, nor did they allude to Salzburg; and during the four days which concluded the stay in Venice Swithin went about with his head up, but his eyes half-closed like a dazed man. Only after they had taken ship at Genoa did he show signs of any healthy interest in life, when, finding that a man on board was perpetually strumming, he locked the piano up and pitched the key into the sea.

That winter in London he behaved much as usual, but fits of moroseness would seize on him, during which he was not pleasant to approach.

One evening when he was walking with a friend in Piccadilly, a girl coming from a side-street accosted him in German. Swithin, after staring at her in silence for some seconds, handed her a five-pound note, to the great amazement of his friend; nor could he himself have explained the meaning of this freak of generosity.

Of Rozsi he never heard again....

This, then, was the substance of what he remembered as he lay ill in bed. Stretching out his hand he pressed the bell. His valet appeared, crossing the room like a cat; a Swede, who had been with Swithin many years; a little man with a dried face and fierce moustache, morbidly sharp nerves, and a queer devotion to his master.

Swithin made a feeble gesture. "Adolf," he said, "I'm very bad."

"Yes, sir!"

"Why do you stand there like a cow?" asked Swithin; "can't you see I'm very bad?"

"Yes, sir!" The valet's face twitched as though it masked the dance of obscure emotions.

"I shall feel better after dinner. What time is it?"

"Five o'clock."

"I thought it was more. The afternoons are very long."

"Yes, sir!" Swithin sighed, as though he had expected the consolation of denial.

"Very likely I shall have a nap. Bring up hot water at half-past six and shave me before dinner."

The valet moved towards the door. Swithin raised himself.

"What did Mr. James say to you?"

"He said you ought to have another doctor; two doctors, he said, better than one. He said, also, he would look in again on his way 'home.'"

Swithin grunted, "Umph! What else did he say?"

"He said you didn't take care of yourself."

Swithin glared.

"Has anybody else been to see me?"

The valet turned away his eyes. "Mrs. Thomas Forsyte came last Monday fortnight."

"How long have I been ill?"

"Five weeks on Saturday."

"Do you think I'm very bad?"

Adolf's face was covered suddenly with crow's-feet. "You have no business to ask me question like that! I am not paid, sir, to answer question like that."

Swithin said faintly: "You're a peppery fool! Open a bottle of champagne!"

Adolf took a bottle of champagne—from a cupboard and held nippers to it. He fixed his eyes on Swithin. "The doctor said—"

"Open the bottle!"

"It is not—"

"Open the bottle—or I give you warning."

Adolf removed the cork. He wiped a glass elaborately, filled it, and bore it scrupulously to the bedside. Suddenly twirling his moustaches, he wrung his hands, and burst out: "It is poison."

Swithin grinned faintly. "You foreign fool!" he said. "Get out!"

The valet vanished.

'He forgot himself!' thought Swithin. Slowly he raised the glass, slowly put it back, and sank gasping on his pillows. Almost at once he fell asleep.

He dreamed that he was at his club, sitting after dinner in the crowded smoking-room, with its bright walls and trefoils of light. It was there that he sat every evening, patient, solemn, lonely, and sometimes fell asleep, his square, pale old face nodding to one side. He dreamed that he was gazing at the picture over the fireplace, of an old statesman with a high collar, supremely finished face, and sceptical eyebrows—the picture, smooth, and reticent as sealing-wax, of one who seemed for ever exhaling the narrow wisdom of final judgments. All round him, his fellow members were chattering. Only he himself, the old sick member, was silent. If fellows only knew what it was like to sit by yourself and feel ill all the time! What they were saying he had heard a hundred times. They were talking of investments, of cigars, horses, actresses, machinery. What was that? A foreign patent for cleaning boilers? There was no such thing; boilers couldn't be cleaned, any fool knew that! If an Englishman couldn't clean a boiler, no foreigner could clean one. He appealed to the old statesman's eyes. But for once those eyes seemed hesitating, blurred, wanting in finality. They vanished. In their place were Rozsi's little deep-set eyes, with their wide and far-off look; and as he gazed they seemed to grow bright as steel, and to speak to him. Slowly the whole face grew to be there, floating on the dark background of the picture; it was pink, aloof, unfathomable, enticing, with its fluffy hair and quick lips, just as he had last seen it. "Are you looking for something?" she seemed to say: "I could show you."

"I have everything safe enough," answered Swithin, and in his sleep he groaned.

He felt the touch of fingers on his forehead. 'I'm dreaming,' he thought in his dream.

She had vanished; and far away, from behind the picture, came a sound of footsteps.

Aloud, in his sleep, Swithin muttered: "I've missed it."

Again he heard the rustling of those light footsteps, and close in his ear a sound, like a sob. He awoke; the sob was his own. Great drops of perspiration stood on his forehead. 'What is it?' he thought; 'what have I lost?' Slowly his mind travelled over his investments; he could not think of any single one that was unsafe. What was it, then, that he had lost? Struggling on his pillows, he clutched the wine-glass. His lips touched the wine. 'This isn't the "Heidseck"!' he thought angrily, and before the reality of that displeasure all the dim vision passed away. But as he bent to drink, something snapped, and, with a sigh, Swithin Forsyte died above the bubbles....

When James Forsyte came in again on his way home, the valet, trembling took his hat and stick.

"How's your master?"

"My master is dead, sir!"

"Dead! He can't be! I left him safe an hour ago."

On the bed Swithin's body was doubled like a sack; his hand still grasped the glass.

James Forsyte paused. "Swithin!" he said, and with his hand to his ear he waited for an answer; but none came, and slowly in the glass a last bubble rose and burst.

December 1900.

To

MY SISTER MABEL EDITH REYNOLDS

THE SILENCE

I

In a car of the Naples express a mining expert was diving into a bag for papers. The strong sunlight showed the fine wrinkles on his brown face and the shabbiness of his short, rough beard. A newspaper cutting slipped from his fingers; he picked it up, thinking: 'How the dickens did that get in here?' It was from a colonial print of three years back; and he sat staring, as if in that forlorn slip of yellow paper he had encountered some ghost from his past.

These were the words he read: "We hope that the setback to civilisation, the check to commerce and development, in this promising centre of our colony may be but temporary; and that capital may again come to the rescue. Where one man was successful, others should surely not fail? We are convinced that it only needs...." And the last words: "For what can be sadder than to see the forest spreading its lengthening shadows, like symbols of defeat, over the untenanted dwellings of men; and where was once the merry chatter of human voices, to pass by in the silence...."

On an afternoon, thirteen years before, he had been in the city of London, at one of those emporiums where mining experts perch, before fresh flights, like sea-gulls on some favourite rock. A clerk said to him: "Mr. Scorrier, they are asking for you downstairs—Mr. Hemmings of the New Colliery Company."

Scorrier took up the speaking tube. "Is that you, Mr. Scorrier? I hope you are very well, sir, I am— Hemmings—I am—coming up."

In two minutes he appeared, Christopher Hemmings, secretary of the New Colliery Company, known in the City-behind his back—as "Down-by-the-starn" Hemmings. He grasped Scorrier's hand—the gesture was deferential, yet distinguished. Too handsome, too capable, too important, his figure, the cut of his iron-grey beard, and his intrusively fine eyes, conveyed a continual courteous invitation to inspect their infallibilities. He stood, like a City "Atlas," with his legs apart, his coat-tails gathered in his hands, a whole globe of financial matters deftly balanced on his nose. "Look at me!" he seemed to say. "It's heavy, but how easily I carry it. Not the man to let it down, Sir!"

"I hope I see you well, Mr. Scorrier," he began. "I have come round about our mine. There is a question of a fresh field being opened up—between ourselves, not before it's wanted. I find it difficult to get my Board to take a comprehensive view. In short, the question is: Are you prepared to go out for us, and report on it? The fees will be all right." His left eye closed. "Things have been very—er—dicky; we are going to change our superintendent. I have got little Pippin—you know little Pippin?"

Scorrier murmured, with a feeling of vague resentment: "Oh yes. He's not a mining man!"

Hemmings replied: "We think that he will do." 'Do you?' thought Scorrier; 'that's good of you!'

He had not altogether shaken off a worship he had felt for Pippin—"King" Pippin he was always called, when they had been boys at the Camborne Grammar-school. "King" Pippin! the boy with the bright colour, very bright hair, bright, subtle, elusive eyes, broad shoulders, little stoop in the neck, and a way of moving it quickly like a bird; the boy who was always at the top of everything, and held his head as if looking for something further to be the top of. He remembered how one day "King" Pippin had said to him in his soft way, "Young Scorrie, I'll do your sums for you"; and in answer to his dubious, "Is that all right?" had replied, "Of course—I don't want you to get behind that beast Blake, he's not a Cornishman" (the beast Blake was an Irishman not yet twelve). He remembered, too, an occasion when "King" Pippin with two other boys fought six louts and got a licking, and how Pippin sat for half an hour afterwards, all bloody, his head in his hands, rocking to and fro, and weeping tears of mortification; and how the next day he had sneaked off by himself, and, attacking the same gang, got frightfully mauled a second time.

Thinking of these things he answered curtly: "When shall I start?"

"Down-by-the-starn" Hemmings replied with a sort of fearful sprightliness: "There's a good fellow! I will send instructions; so glad to see you well." Conferring on Scorrier a look—fine to the verge of vulgarity—he withdrew. Scorrier remained, seated; heavy with insignificance and vague oppression, as if he had drunk a tumbler of sweet port.

A week later, in company with Pippin, he was on board a liner.

The "King" Pippin of his school-days was now a man of forty-four. He awakened in Scorrier the uncertain wonder with which men look backward at their uncomplicated teens; and staggering up and down the decks in the long Atlantic roll, he would steal glances at his companion, as if he expected to find out from them something about himself. Pippin had still "King" Pippin's bright, fine hair, and dazzling streaks in his short beard; he had still a bright colour and suave voice, and what there were of wrinkles suggested only subtleties of humour and ironic sympathy. From the first, and apparently without negotiation, he had his seat at the captain's table, to which on the second day Scorrier too found himself translated, and had to sit, as he expressed it ruefully, "among the big-wigs."

During the voyage only one incident impressed itself on Scorrier's memory, and that for a disconcerting reason. In the forecastle were the usual complement of emigrants. One evening, leaning across the rail to watch them, he felt a touch on his arm; and, looking round, saw Pippin's face and beard quivering in the lamplight. "Poor people!" he said. The idea flashed on Scorrier that he was like some fine wire sound-recording instrument.

'Suppose he were to snap!' he thought. Impelled to justify this fancy, he blurted out: "You're a nervous chap. The way you look at those poor devils!"

Pippin hustled him along the deck. "Come, come, you took me off my guard," he murmured, with a sly, gentle smile, "that's not fair."

He found it a continual source of wonder that Pippin, at his age, should cut himself adrift from the associations and security of London life to begin a new career in a new country with dubious prospect of success. 'I always heard he was doing well all round,' he thought; 'thinks he'll better himself, perhaps. He's a true Cornishman.'

The morning of arrival at the mines was grey and cheerless; a cloud of smoke, beaten down by drizzle, clung above the forest; the wooden houses straggled dismally in the unkempt semblance of a street, against a background of endless, silent woods. An air of blank discouragement brooded over everything; cranes jutted idly over empty trucks; the long jetty oozed black slime; miners with listless faces stood in the rain; dogs fought under their very legs. On the way to the hotel they met no one busy or serene except a Chinee who was polishing a dish-cover.

The late superintendent, a cowed man, regaled them at lunch with his forebodings; his attitude toward the situation was like the food, which was greasy and uninspiring. Alone together once more, the two newcomers eyed each other sadly.

"Oh dear!" sighed Pippin. "We must change all this, Scorrier; it will never do to go back beaten. I shall not go back beaten; you will have to carry me on my shield;" and slyly: "Too heavy, eh? Poor fellow!" Then for a long time he was silent, moving his lips as if adding up the cost. Suddenly he sighed, and grasping Scorrier's arm, said: "Dull, aren't I? What will you do? Put me in your report, 'New Superintendent—sad, dull dog—not a word to throw at a cat!'" And as if the new task were too much for him, he sank back in thought. The last words he said to Scorrier that night were: "Very silent here. It's hard to believe one's here for life. But I feel I am. Mustn't be a coward, though!" and brushing his forehead, as though to clear from it a cobweb of faint thoughts, he hurried off.

Scorrier stayed on the veranda smoking. The rain had ceased, a few stars were burning dimly; even above the squalor of the township the scent of the forests, the interminable forests, brooded. There sprang into his mind the memory of a picture from one of his children's fairy books—the picture of a little bearded man on tiptoe, with poised head and a great sword, slashing at the castle of a giant. It reminded him of Pippin. And suddenly, even to Scorrier—whose existence was one long encounter with strange places—the unseen presence of those woods, their heavy, healthy scent, the little sounds, like squeaks from tiny toys, issuing out of the gloomy silence, seemed intolerable, to be shunned, from the mere instinct of self-preservation. He thought of the evening he had spent in the bosom of "Down-by-the-starn" Hemmings' family, receiving his last instructions—the security of that suburban villa, its discouraging gentility; the superior acidity of the Miss Hemmings; the noble names of large contractors, of company promoters, of a peer, dragged with the lightness of gun-carriages across the conversation; the autocracy of Hemmings, rasped up here and there, by some domestic contradiction. It was all so nice and safe—as if the whole thing had been fastened to an anchor sunk beneath the pink cabbages of the drawing-room carpet! Hemmings, seeing him off the premises, had said with secrecy: "Little Pippin will have a good thing. We shall make his salary L——. He'll be a great man-quite a king. Ha-ha!"

Scorrier shook the ashes from his pipe. 'Salary!' he thought, straining his ears; 'I wouldn't take the place for five thousand pounds a year. And yet it's a fine country,' and with ironic violence he repeated, 'a dashed fine country!'

Ten days later, having finished his report on the new mine, he stood on the jetty waiting to go abroad the steamer for home.

"God bless you!" said Pippin. "Tell them they needn't be afraid; and sometimes when you're at home think of me, eh?"

Scorrier, scrambling on board, had a confused memory of tears in his eyes, and a convulsive handshake.

II

It was eight years before the wheels of life carried Scorrier back to that disenchanted spot, and this time not on the business of the New Colliery Company. He went for another company with a mine some thirty miles away. Before starting, however, he visited Hemmings. The secretary was surrounded by pigeon-holes and finer than ever; Scorrier blinked in the full radiance of his courtesy. A little man with eyebrows full of questions, and a grizzled beard, was seated in an arm-chair by the fire.

"You know Mr. Booker," said Hemmings—"one of my directors. This is Mr. Scorrier, sir—who went out for us."

These sentences were murmured in a way suggestive of their uncommon value. The director uncrossed his legs, and bowed. Scorrier also bowed, and Hemmings, leaning back, slowly developed the full resources of his waistcoat.

"So you are going out again, Scorrier, for the other side? I tell Mr. Scorrier, sir, that he is going out for the enemy. Don't find them a mine as good as you found us, there's a good man."

The little director asked explosively: "See our last dividend? Twenty per cent; eh, what?"

Hemmings moved a finger, as if reproving his director. "I will not disguise from you," he murmured, "that there is friction between us and—the enemy; you know our position too well—just a little too well, eh? 'A nod's as good as a wink.'"

His diplomatic eyes flattered Scorrier, who passed a hand over his brow—and said: "Of course."

"Pippin doesn't hit it off with them. Between ourselves, he's a leetle too big for his boots. You know what it is when a man in his position gets a sudden rise!"

Scorrier caught himself searching on the floor for a sight of Hemmings' boots; he raised his eyes guiltily. The secretary continued: "We don't hear from him quite as often as we should like, in fact."

To his own surprise Scorrier murmured: "It's a silent place!"

The secretary smiled. "Very good! Mr. Scorrier says, sir, it's a silent place; ha-ha! I call that very good!" But suddenly a secret irritation seemed to bubble in him; he burst forth almost violently: "He's no business to let it affect him; now, has he? I put it to you, Mr. Scorrier, I put it to you, sir!"

But Scorrier made no reply, and soon after took his leave: he had been asked to convey a friendly hint to Pippin that more frequent letters would be welcomed. Standing in the shadow of the Royal Exchange, waiting to thread his way across, he thought: 'So you must have noise, must you—you've got some here, and to spare....'

On his arrival in the new world he wired to Pippin asking if he might stay with him on the way up country, and received the answer: "Be sure and come."

A week later he arrived (there was now a railway) and found Pippin waiting for him in a phaeton. Scorrier would not have known the place again; there was a glitter over everything, as if some one had touched it with a wand. The tracks had given place to roads, running firm, straight, and black between the trees under brilliant sunshine; the wooden houses were all painted; out in the gleaming harbour amongst the green of islands lay three steamers, each with a fleet of busy boats; and here and there a tiny yacht floated, like a sea-bird on the water. Pippin drove his long-tailed horses furiously; his eyes brimmed with subtle kindness, as if according Scorrier a continual welcome. During the two days of his stay Scorrier never lost that sense of glamour. He had every opportunity for observing the grip Pippin had over everything. The wooden doors and walls of his bungalow kept out no sounds. He listened to interviews between his host and all kinds and conditions of men. The voices of the visitors would rise at first—angry, discontented, matter-of-fact, with nasal twang, or guttural drawl; then would come the soft patter of the superintendent's feet crossing and recrossing the room. Then a pause, the sound of hard breathing, and quick questions—the visitor's voice again, again the patter, and Pippin's ingratiating but decisive murmurs. Presently out would come the visitor with an expression on his face which Scorrier soon began to know by heart, a kind of pleased, puzzled, helpless look, which seemed to say, "I've been done, I know—I'll give it to myself when I'm round the corner."

Pippin was full of wistful questions about "home." He wanted to talk of music, pictures, plays, of how London looked, what new streets there were, and, above all, whether Scorrier had been lately in the West Country. He talked of getting leave next winter, asked whether Scorrier thought they would "put up with him at home"; then, with the agitation which had alarmed Scorrier before, he added: "Ah! but I'm not fit for home now. One gets spoiled; it's big and silent here. What should I go back to? I don't seem to realise."

Scorrier thought of Hemmings. "'Tis a bit cramped there, certainly," he muttered.

Pippin went on as if divining his thoughts. "I suppose our friend Hemmings would call me foolish; he's above the little weaknesses of imagination, eh? Yes; it's silent here. Sometimes in the evening I would give my head for somebody to talk to—Hemmings would never give his head for anything, I think. But all the same, I couldn't face them at home. Spoiled!" And slyly he murmured: "What would the Board say if they could hear that?"

Scorrier blurted out: "To tell you the truth, they complain a little of not hearing from you."

Pippin put out a hand, as if to push something away. "Let them try the life here!" he broke out; "it's like sitting on a live volcano—what with our friends, 'the enemy,' over there; the men; the American competition. I keep it going, Scorrier, but at what a cost—at what a cost!"

"But surely—letters?"

Pippin only answered: "I try—I try!"

Scorrier felt with remorse and wonder that he had spoken the truth. The following day he left for his inspection, and while in the camp of "the enemy" much was the talk he heard of Pippin.

"Why!" said his host, the superintendent, a little man with a face somewhat like an owl's, "d'you know the name they've given him down in the capital—'the King'—good, eh? He's made them 'sit up' all along this coast. I like him well enough—good—hearted man, shocking nervous; but my people down there can't stand him at any price. Sir, he runs this colony. You'd think butter wouldn't melt in that mouth of his; but he always gets his way; that's what riles 'em so; that and the success he's making of his mine. It puzzles me; you'd think he'd only be too glad of a quiet life, a man with his nerves. But no, he's never happy unless he's fighting, something where he's got a chance to score a victory. I won't say he likes it, but, by Jove, it seems he's got to do it. Now that's funny! I'll tell you one thing, though shouldn't be a bit surprised if he broke down some day; and I'll tell you another," he added darkly, "he's sailing very near the wind, with those large contracts that he makes. I wouldn't care to take his risks. Just let them have a strike, or something that shuts them down for a spell—and mark my words, sir—it'll be all up with them. But," he concluded confidentially, "I wish I had his hold on the men; it's a great thing in this country. Not like home, where you can go round a corner and get another gang. You have to make the best you can out of the lot you have; you won't, get another man for love or money without you ship him a few hundred miles." And with a frown he waved his arm over the forests to indicate the barrenness of the land.

III

Scorrier finished his inspection and went on a shooting trip into the forest. His host met him on his return. "Just look at this!" he said, holding out a telegram. "Awful, isn't it?" His face expressed a profound commiseration, almost ludicrously mixed with the ashamed contentment that men experience at the misfortunes of an enemy.

The telegram, dated the day before, ran thus "Frightful explosion New Colliery this morning, great loss of life feared."

Scorrier had the bewildered thought: 'Pippin will want me now.'

He took leave of his host, who called after him: "You'd better wait for a steamer! It's a beastly drive!"

Scorrier shook his head. All night, jolting along a rough track cut through the forest, he thought of Pippin. The other miseries of this calamity at present left him cold; he barely thought of the smothered men; but Pippin's struggle, his lonely struggle with this hydra-headed monster, touched him very nearly. He fell asleep and dreamed of watching Pippin slowly strangled by a snake; the agonised, kindly, ironic face peeping out between two gleaming coils was so horribly real, that he awoke. It was the moment before dawn: pitch-black branches barred the sky; with every jolt of the wheels the gleams from the lamps danced, fantastic and intrusive, round ferns and tree-stems, into the cold heart of the forest. For an hour or more Scorrier tried to feign sleep, and hide from the stillness, and overmastering gloom of these great woods. Then softly a whisper of noises stole forth, a stir of light, and the whole slow radiance of the morning glory. But it brought no warmth; and Scorrier wrapped himself closer in his cloak, feeling as though old age had touched him.

Close on noon he reached the township. Glamour seemed still to hover over it. He drove on to the mine. The winding-engine was turning, the pulley at the top of the head-gear whizzing round; nothing looked unusual. 'Some mistake!' he thought. He drove to the mine buildings, alighted, and climbed to the shaft head. Instead of the usual rumbling of the trolleys, the rattle of coal discharged over the screens, there was silence. Close by, Pippin himself was standing, smirched with dirt. The cage, coming swift and silent from below, shot open its doors with a sharp rattle. Scorrier bent forward to look. There lay a dead man, with a smile on his face.

"How many?" he whispered.

Pippin answered: "Eighty-four brought up—forty-seven still below," and entered the man's name in a pocket-book.

An older man was taken out next; he too was smiling—there had been vouchsafed to him, it seemed, a taste of more than earthly joy. The sight of those strange smiles affected Scorrier more than all the anguish or despair he had seen scored on the faces of other dead men. He asked an old miner how long Pippin had been at work.

"Thirty hours. Yesterday he wer' below; we had to nigh carry mun up at last. He's for goin' down again, but the chaps won't lower mun;" the old man gave a sigh. "I'm waiting for my boy to come up, I am."

Scorrier waited too—there was fascination about those dead, smiling faces. The rescuing of these men who would never again breathe went on and on. Scorrier grew sleepy in the sun. The old miner woke him, saying: "Rummy stuff this here chokedamp; see, they all dies drunk!" The very next to be brought up was the chief engineer. Scorrier had known him quite well, one of those Scotsmen who are born at the age of forty and remain so all their lives. His face—the only one that wore no smile—seemed grieving that duty had deprived it of that last luxury. With wide eyes and drawn lips he had died protesting.

Late in the afternoon the old miner touched Scorrier's arm, and said: "There he is—there's my boy!" And he departed slowly, wheeling the body on a trolley.

As the sun set, the gang below came up. No further search was possible till the fumes had cleared. Scorrier heard one man say: "There's some we'll never get; they've had sure burial."

Another answered him: "'Tis a gude enough bag for me!" They passed him, the whites of their eyes gleaming out of faces black as ink.

Pippin drove him home at a furious pace, not uttering a single word. As they turned into the main street, a young woman starting out before the horses obliged Pippin to pull up. The glance he bent on Scorrier was ludicrously prescient of suffering. The woman asked for her husband. Several times they were stopped thus by women asking for their husbands or sons. "This is what I have to go through," Pippin whispered.

When they had eaten, he said to Scorrier: "It was kind of you to come and stand by me! They take me for a god, poor creature that I am. But shall I ever get the men down again? Their nerve's shaken. I wish I were one of those poor lads, to die with a smile like that!"

Scorrier felt the futility of his presence. On Pippin alone must be the heat and burden. Would he stand under it, or would the whole thing come crashing to the ground? He urged him again and again to rest, but Pippin only gave him one of his queer smiles. "You don't know how strong I am!" he said.

IV

He himself slept heavily; and, waking at dawn, went down. Pippin was still at his desk; his pen had dropped; he was asleep. The ink was wet; Scorrier's eye caught the opening words:

"GENTLEMEN,—Since this happened I have not slept...."

He stole away again with a sense of indignation that no one could be dragged in to share that fight. The London Board-room rose before his mind. He imagined the portentous gravity of Hemmings; his face and voice and manner conveying the impression that he alone could save the situation; the six directors, all men of commonsense and certainly humane, seated behind large turret-shaped inkpots; the concern and irritation in their voices, asking how it could have happened; their comments: "An awful thing!" "I suppose Pippin is doing the best he can!" "Wire him on no account to leave the mine idle!" "Poor devils!" "A fund? Of course, what ought we to give?" He had a strong conviction that nothing of all this would disturb the commonsense with which they would go home and eat their mutton. A good thing too; the less it was taken to heart the better! But Scorrier felt angry. The fight was so unfair! A fellow all nerves—with not a soul to help him! Well, it was his own lookout! He had chosen to centre it all in himself, to make himself its very soul. If he gave way now, the ship must go down! By a thin thread, Scorrier's hero-worship still held. 'Man against nature,' he thought, 'I back the man.' The struggle in which he was so powerless to give aid, became intensely personal to him, as if he had engaged his own good faith therein.

The next day they went down again to the pit-head; and Scorrier himself descended. The fumes had almost cleared, but there were some places which would never be reached. At the end of the day all but four bodies had been recovered. "In the day o' judgment," a miner said, "they four'll come out of here." Those unclaimed bodies haunted Scorrier. He came on sentences of writing, where men waiting to be suffocated had written down their feelings. In one place, the hour, the word "Sleepy," and a signature. In another, "A. F.—done for." When he came up at last Pippin was still waiting, pocket-book in hand; they again departed at a furious pace.

Two days later Scorrier, visiting the shaft, found its neighbourhood deserted—not a living thing of any sort was there except one Chinaman poking his stick into the rubbish. Pippin was away down the coast engaging an engineer; and on his return, Scorrier had not the heart to tell him of the desertion. He was spared the effort, for Pippin said: "Don't be afraid—you've got bad news? The men have gone on strike."

Scorrier sighed. "Lock, stock, and barrel"

"I thought so—see what I have here!" He put before Scorrier a telegram:

"At all costs keep working—fatal to stop—manage this somehow.—HEMMINGS."

Breathing quickly, he added: "As if I didn't know! 'Manage this somehow'—a little hard!"

"What's to be done?" asked Scorrier.

"You see I am commanded!" Pippin answered bitterly. "And they're quite right; we must keep working—our contracts! Now I'm down—not a soul will spare me!"

The miners' meeting was held the following day on the outskirts of the town. Pippin had cleared the place to make a public recreation-ground—a sort of feather in the company's cap; it was now to be the spot whereon should be decided the question of the company's life or death.

The sky to the west was crossed by a single line of cloud like a bar of beaten gold; tree shadows crept towards the groups of men; the evening savour, that strong fragrance of the forest, sweetened the air. The miners stood all round amongst the burnt tree-stumps, cowed and sullen. They looked incapable of movement or expression. It was this dumb paralysis that frightened Scorrier. He watched Pippin speaking from his phaeton, the butt of all those sullen, restless eyes. Would he last out? Would the wires hold? It was like the finish of a race. He caught a baffled look on Pippin's face, as if he despaired of piercing that terrible paralysis. The men's eyes had begun to wander. 'He's lost his hold,' thought Scorrier; 'it's all up!'

A miner close beside him muttered: "Look out!"

Pippin was leaning forward, his voice had risen, the words fell like a whiplash on the faces of the crowd: "You shan't throw me over; do you think I'll give up all I've done for you? I'll make you the first power in the colony! Are you turning tail at the first shot? You're a set of cowards, my lads!"

Each man round Scorrier was listening with a different motion of the hands—one rubbed them, one clenched them, another moved his closed fist, as if stabbing some one in the back. A grisly-bearded, beetle-browed, twinkling-eyed old Cornishman muttered: "A'hm not troublin' about that." It seemed almost as if Pippin's object was to get the men to kill him; they had gathered closer, crouching for a rush. Suddenly Pippin's voice dropped to a whisper: "I'm disgraced Men, are you going back on me?"

The old miner next Scorrier called out suddenly: "Anny that's Cornishmen here to stand by the superintendent?" A group drew together, and with murmurs and gesticulation the meeting broke up.

In the evening a deputation came to visit Pippin; and all night long their voices and the superintendent's footsteps could be heard. In the morning, Pippin went early to the mine. Before supper the deputation came again; and again Scorrier had to listen hour after hour to the sound of voices and footsteps till he fell asleep. Just before dawn he was awakened by a light. Pippin stood at his bedside. "The men go down to-morrow," he said: "What did I tell you? Carry me home on my shield, eh?"

In a week the mine was in full work.

V

Two years later, Scorrier heard once more of Pippin. A note from Hemmings reached him asking if he could make it convenient to attend their Board meeting the following Thursday. He arrived rather before the appointed time. The secretary received him, and, in answer to inquiry, said: "Thank you, we are doing well—between ourselves, we are doing very well."

"And Pippin?"

The secretary frowned. "Ah, Pippin! We asked you to come on his account. Pippin is giving us a lot of trouble. We have not had a single line from him for just two years!" He spoke with such a sense of personal grievance that Scorrier felt quite sorry for him. "Not a single line," said Hemmings, "since that explosion—you were there at the time, I remember! It makes it very awkward; I call it personal to me."

"But how—" Scorrier began.

"We get—telegrams. He writes to no one, not even to his family. And why? Just tell me why? We hear of him; he's a great nob out there. Nothing's done in the colony without his finger being in the pie. He turned out the last Government because they wouldn't grant us an extension for our railway—shows he can't be a fool. Besides, look at our balance-sheet!"

It turned out that the question on which Scorrier's opinion was desired was, whether Hemmings should be sent out to see what was the matter with the superintendent. During the discussion which ensued, he was an unwilling listener to strictures on Pippin's silence. "The explosion," he muttered at last, "a very trying time!"

Mr. Booker pounced on him. "A very trying time! So it was—to all of us. But what excuse is that—now, Mr. Scorrier, what excuse is that?"

Scorrier was obliged to admit that it was none.

"Business is business—eh, what?"

Scorrier, gazing round that neat Board-room, nodded. A deaf director, who had not spoken for some months, said with sudden fierceness: "It's disgraceful!" He was obviously letting off the fume of long-unuttered disapprovals. One perfectly neat, benevolent old fellow, however, who had kept his hat on, and had a single vice—that of coming to the Board-room with a brown paper parcel tied up with string—murmured: "We must make all allowances," and started an anecdote about his youth. He was gently called to order by his secretary. Scorrier was asked for his opinion. He looked at Hemmings. "My importance is concerned," was written all over the secretary's face. Moved by an impulse of loyalty to Pippin, Scorrier answered, as if it were all settled: "Well, let me know when you are starting, Hemmings—I should like the trip myself."

As he was going out, the chairman, old Jolyon Forsyte, with a grave, twinkling look at Hemmings, took him aside. "Glad to hear you say that about going too, Mr. Scorrier; we must be careful—Pippin's such a good fellow, and so sensitive; and our friend there—a bit heavy in the hand, um?"

Scorrier did in fact go out with Hemmings. The secretary was sea-sick, and his prostration, dignified but noisy, remained a memory for ever; it was sonorous and fine—the prostration of superiority; and the way in which he spoke of it, taking casual acquaintances into the caves of his experience, was truly interesting.

Pippin came down to the capital to escort them, provided for their comforts as if they had been royalty, and had a special train to take them to the mines.

He was a little stouter, brighter of colour, greyer of beard, more nervous perhaps in voice and breathing. His manner to Hemmings was full of flattering courtesy; but his sly, ironical glances played on the secretary's armour like a fountain on a hippopotamus. To Scorrier, however, he could not show enough affection:

The first evening, when Hemmings had gone to his room, he jumped up like a boy out of school. "So I'm going to get a wigging," he said; "I suppose I deserve it; but if you knew—if you only knew...! Out here they've nicknamed me 'the King'—they say I rule the colony. It's myself that I can't rule"; and with a sudden burst of passion such as Scorrier had never seen in him: "Why did they send this man here? What can he know about the things that I've been through?" In a moment he calmed down again. "There! this is very stupid; worrying you like this!" and with a long, kind look into Scorrier's face, he hustled him off to bed.

Pippin did not break out again, though fire seemed to smoulder behind the bars of his courteous irony. Intuition of danger had evidently smitten Hemmings, for he made no allusion to the object of his visit. There were moments when Scorrier's common-sense sided with Hemmings—these were moments when the secretary was not present.

'After all,' he told himself, 'it's a little thing to ask—one letter a month. I never heard of such a case.' It was wonderful indeed how they stood it! It showed how much they valued Pippin! What was the matter with him? What was the nature of his trouble? One glimpse Scorrier had when even Hemmings, as he phrased it, received "quite a turn." It was during a drive back from the most outlying of the company's trial mines, eight miles through the forest. The track led through a belt of trees blackened by a forest fire. Pippin was driving. The secretary seated beside him wore an expression of faint alarm, such as Pippin's driving was warranted to evoke from almost any face. The sky had darkened strangely, but pale streaks of light, coming from one knew not where, filtered through the trees. No breath was stirring; the wheels and horses' hoofs made no sound on the deep fern mould. All around, the burnt tree-trunks, leafless and jagged, rose like withered giants, the passages between them were black, the sky black, and black the silence. No one spoke, and literally the only sound was Pippin's breathing. What was it that was so terrifying? Scorrier had a feeling of entombment; that nobody could help him; the feeling of being face to face with Nature; a sensation as if all the comfort and security of words and rules had dropped away from him. And-nothing happened. They reached home and dined.

During dinner he had again that old remembrance of a little man chopping at a castle with his sword. It came at a moment when Pippin had raised his hand with the carving-knife grasped in it to answer some remark of Hemmings' about the future of the company. The optimism in his uplifted chin, the strenuous energy in his whispering voice, gave Scorrier a more vivid glimpse of Pippin's nature than he had perhaps ever had before. This new country, where nothing but himself could help a man— that was the castle! No wonder Pippin was impatient of control, no wonder he was out of hand, no wonder he was silent—chopping away at that! And suddenly he thought: 'Yes, and all the time one knows, Nature must beat him in the end!'

That very evening Hemmings delivered himself of his reproof. He had sat unusually silent; Scorrier, indeed, had thought him a little drunk, so portentous was his gravity; suddenly, however he rose. It was hard on a man, he said, in his position, with a Board (he spoke as of a family of small children), to be kept so short of information. He was actually compelled to use his imagination to answer the shareholders' questions. This was painful and humiliating; he had never heard of any secretary having to use his imagination! He went further—it was insulting! He had grown grey in the service of the company. Mr. Scorrier would bear him out when he said he had a position to maintain—his name in the City was a high one; and, by George! he was going to keep it a high one; he would allow nobody to drag it in the dust—that ought clearly to be understood. His directors felt they were being treated like children; however that might be, it was absurd to suppose that he (Hemmings) could be treated like a child...! The secretary paused; his eyes seemed to bully the room.

"If there were no London office," murmured Pippin, "the shareholders would get the same dividends."

Hemmings gasped. "Come!" he said, "this is monstrous!"

"What help did I get from London when I first came here? What help have I ever had?"

Hemmings swayed, recovered, and with a forced smile replied that, if this were true, he had been standing on his head for years; he did not believe the attitude possible for such a length of time; personally he would have thought that he too had had a little something to say to the company's position, but no matter...! His irony was crushing.... It was possible that Mr. Pippin hoped to reverse the existing laws of the universe with regard to limited companies; he would merely say that he must not begin with a company of which he (Hemmings) happened to be secretary. Mr. Scorrier had hinted at excuses; for his part, with the best intentions in the world, he had great difficulty in seeing them. He would go further—he did not see them! The explosion...! Pippin shrank so visibly that Hemmings seemed troubled by a suspicion that he had gone too far.

"We know," he said, "that it was trying for you...."

"Trying!" "burst out Pippin.

"No one can say," Hemmings resumed soothingly, "that we have not dealt liberally." Pippin made a motion of the head. "We think we have a good superintendent; I go further, an excellent superintendent. What I say is: Let's be pleasant! I am not making an unreasonable request!" He ended on a fitting note of jocularity; and, as if by consent, all three withdrew, each to his own room, without another word.

In the course of the next day Pippin said to Scorrier: "It seems I have been very wicked. I must try to do better"; and with a touch of bitter humour, "They are kind enough to think me a good superintendent, you see! After that I must try hard."

Scorrier broke in: "No man could have done so much for them;" and, carried away by an impulse to put things absolutely straight, went on "But, after all, a letter now and then—what does it amount to?"

Pippin besieged him with a subtle glance. "You too?" he said—"I must indeed have been a wicked man!" and turned away.

Scorrier felt as if he had been guilty of brutality; sorry for Pippin, angry with himself; angry with Pippin, sorry for himself. He earnestly desired to see the back of Hemmings. The secretary gratified the wish a few days later, departing by steamer with ponderous expressions of regard and the assurance of his goodwill.

Pippin gave vent to no outburst of relief, maintaining a courteous silence, making only one allusion to his late guest, in answer to a remark of Scorrier:

"Ah! don't tempt me! mustn't speak behind his back."

VI

A month passed, and Scorrier still—remained Pippin's guest. As each mail-day approached he experienced a queer suppressed excitement. On one of these occasions Pippin had withdrawn to his room; and when Scorrier went to fetch him to dinner he found him with his head leaning on his hands, amid a perfect fitter of torn paper. He looked up at Scorrier.

"I can't do it," he said, "I feel such a hypocrite; I can't put myself into leading-strings again. Why should I ask these people, when I've settled everything already? If it were a vital matter they wouldn't want to hear—they'd simply wire, 'Manage this somehow!'"

Scorrier said nothing, but thought privately 'This is a mad business!' What was a letter? Why make a fuss about a letter? The approach of mail-day seemed like a nightmare to the superintendent; he became feverishly nervous like a man under a spell; and, when the mail had gone, behaved like a respited criminal. And this had been going on two years! Ever since that explosion. Why, it was monomania!

One day, a month after Hemmings' departure, Pippin rose early from dinner; his face was flushed, he had been drinking wine. "I won't be beaten this time," he said, as he passed Scorrier. The latter could hear him writing in the next room, and looked in presently to say that he was going for a walk. Pippin gave him a kindly nod.

It was a cool, still evening: innumerable stars swarmed in clusters over the forests, forming bright hieroglyphics in the middle heavens, showering over the dark harbour into the sea. Scorrier walked slowly. A weight seemed lifted from his mind, so entangled had he become in that uncanny silence. At last Pippin had broken through the spell. To get that, letter sent would be the laying of a phantom, the rehabilitation of commonsense. Now that this silence was in the throes of being broken, he felt curiously tender towards Pippin, without the hero-worship of old days, but with a queer protective feeling. After all, he was different from other men. In spite of his feverish, tenacious energy, in spite of his ironic humour, there was something of the woman in him! And as for this silence, this horror of control—all geniuses had "bees in their bonnets," and Pippin was a genius in his way!

He looked back at the town. Brilliantly lighted it had a thriving air-difficult to believe of the place he remembered ten years back; the sounds of drinking, gambling, laughter, and dancing floated to his ears. 'Quite a city!' he thought.

With this queer elation on him he walked slowly back along the street, forgetting that he was simply an oldish mining expert, with a look of shabbiness, such as clings to men who are always travelling, as if their "nap" were for ever being rubbed off. And he thought of Pippin, creator of this glory.

He had passed the boundaries of the town, and had entered the forest. A feeling of discouragement instantly beset him. The scents and silence, after the festive cries and odours of the town, were undefinably oppressive. Notwithstanding, he walked a long time, saying to himself that he would give the letter every chance. At last, when he thought that Pippin must have finished, he went back to the house.

Pippin had finished. His forehead rested on the table, his arms hung at his sides; he was stone-dead! His face wore a smile, and by his side lay an empty laudanum bottle.

The letter, closely, beautifully written, lay before him. It was a fine document, clear, masterly, detailed, nothing slurred, nothing concealed, nothing omitted; a complete review of the company's position; it ended with the words: "Your humble servant, RICHARD PIPPIN."

Scorrier took possession of it. He dimly understood that with those last words a wire had snapped. The border-line had been overpassed; the point reached where that sense of proportion, which alone makes life possible, is lost. He was certain that at the moment of his death Pippin could have discussed bimetallism, or any intellectual problem, except the one problem of his own heart; that, for some mysterious reason, had been too much for him. His death had been the work of a moment of supreme revolt—a single instant of madness on a single subject! He found on the blotting-paper, scrawled across the impress of the signature, "Can't stand it!" The completion of that letter had been to him a struggle ungraspable by Scorrier. Slavery? Defeat? A violation of Nature? The death of justice? It were better not to think of it! Pippin could have told—but he would never speak again. Nature, at whom, unaided, he had dealt so many blows, had taken her revenge...!

In the night Scorrier stole down, and, with an ashamed face, cut off a lock of the fine grey hair. 'His daughter might like it!' he thought....

He waited till Pippin was buried, then, with the letter in his pocket, started for England.

He arrived at Liverpool on a Thursday morning, and travelling to town, drove straight to the office of the company. The Board were sitting. Pippin's successor was already being interviewed. He passed out as Scorrier came in, a middle-aged man with a large, red beard, and a foxy, compromising face. He also was a Cornishman. Scorrier wished him luck with a very heavy heart.

As an unsentimental man, who had a proper horror of emotion, whose living depended on his good sense, to look back on that interview with the Board was painful. It had excited in him a rage of which he was now heartily ashamed. Old Jolyon Forsyte, the chairman, was not there for once, guessing perhaps that the Board's view of this death would be too small for him; and little Mr. Booker sat in his place. Every one had risen, shaken hands with Scorrier, and expressed themselves indebted for his coming. Scorrier placed Pippin's letter on the table, and gravely the secretary read out to his Board the last words of their superintendent. When he had finished, a director said, "That's not the letter of a madman!" Another answered: "Mad as a hatter; nobody but a madman would have thrown up such a post." Scorrier suddenly withdrew. He heard Hemmings calling after him. "Aren't you well, Mr. Scorrier? aren't you well, sir?"

He shouted back: "Quite sane, I thank you...."

The Naples "express" rolled round the outskirts of the town. Vesuvius shone in the sun, uncrowned by smoke. But even as Scorrier looked, a white puff went soaring up. It was the footnote to his memories.

February 1901. February 1901.

John Galsworthy – His Life And Times

John Galsworthy, eldest son of John Galsworthy (1817-1904), a solicitor and company director of Old Jewry, London, and Blanche Bailey (1835-1915), daughter of Charles Bartleet, a needlemaker in Redditch. His father's ancestors originated in Wembury, near Plymouth in England, and Galsworthy, for whom family origins were of significant importance, maintained a close connection with Devon. His more immediate family were considerably wealthy and well established in the shipping industry, and owned a fine estate in Kingston-upon-Thames called Parkfield, where Galsworthy was born on the 14th August 1867. At the age of nine he began education at Saugeen, a Bournemouth preparatory school, before starting at Harrow school in 1881 where he remained until 1886, distinguishing himself as an athlete.

His education at Harrow being successful enough to gain him entrance to Oxford, he began at New College to read law and gained a second-class degree with honours in 1889. Following Lincoln's Inn he was called to the bar in 1890. Despite this recognition he realised that he was not keen to actually begin practising law and so he resolved instead to look after the family's shipping business while specialising himself in Marine Law. This decision saw him take to the seas to destinations such as Vancouver, Island and South AFrica, though it was at the age of twenty-five on one particular journey to Australia, motivated by an (unfulfilled) intention to meet Robert Louis Stevenson on Samoa that he would being to realise fully his literary interests: though he was not considering becoming a writer at this time, his enjoyment of literature was enough to encourage an attempt at meeting a great writer and eventually enabled one of the most significant encounters of his life. He made the journey with his friend Edward Sanderson and, though he missed Stevenson, he met Joseph Conrad, a fellow future author famed for his novels which were often nautically themed. At the time Conrad was the first mate of the sailing-ship Torrens moored in the harbour of Adelaide, Australia; still very much focused on his ship-borne career, he was yet to begin his writing in earnest.

Indeed, though neither knew at the time, both Conrad and Galsworthy were at similar junctures in their lives, their time spent as sea acting as a transitional period during which each found their literary calling. It is perhaps owning to this unknown common ground that they became close friends. During his time on the Torrens Galsworthy recorded several details, offering a frank and valuable characterisation of Conrad while also illuminating his own experiences as a student of Marine Law.

"I supposed to be studying navigation for the Admiralty Bar, would every day work out the position of the ship with the captain. On one side of the saloon table we would sit and check our observations with those of Conrad, who from the other side of the table would look at us a little quizzically."

On his return to England and the cessation of his nautical voyaging, Galsworthy began an affair with the wife of his first cousin, Major Arthur John Galsworthy. Ada Nemesis Pearson Cooper (1864-1956), the daughter of Emanuel Copper, an obstetrician from Norwich, remained married to the Major for ten years and the affair remained secret for its duration. In order to conceal the affair they took considerable pains to avoid suspicion. One such tactic was to stay in a secluded farmhouse called Wingstone in the village on Manaton on Dartmoor, in Devon. In Galsworthy's decision to choose Devon as the location for their clandestine rendezvous we see evidence of Galsworthy's affection for the place of his father's origin. It was only when, in 1905, she divorced the Major that their affair became known following their marriage on 23rd September of that year.

Galsworthy now took to writing sometime after having met Conrad and his career began in earnest when, in 1897, his first work, From the Four Winds, a volume of short stories, was published under the pseudonym John Sinjohn. He succeeded this in 1898 with Jocelyn, his first novel, and then his second in 1900, Villa Rubein. In 1901 he published a second volume of short stories, A Man of Devon, which was the last of his work to be published under pseudonym. The first of his work to be published under his own name was The Island Pharisees in 1904, a novel of social observation, seasoned with flashes of satire and propaganda. His decision to write under his own name is arguably owing to the recent death of his father, either as a mark of respect to his name or because now he was able to publish freely without incurring the possibility of paternal disappointment at his choice of career. It also marked a shift in his professionalism; he had hitherto published with small, independent publishers, but The Island Pharisees was published by Heinemann, a far more established House and one with whom he remained for the duration of his writing career.

He arguably cemented his position and maturity as a writer when, in 1906, he saw the publication of both his first major play, The Silver Box, and the novel The Man of Property. Each was published to considerable critical acclaim, and to achieve both in such a short space of time was impressive. The Silver Box concerns the imbalance in the justice system with regards to criminals of differing class by contrasting the treatment of a poor thief and a rich thief, both of whom stole silver cigarette cases but for very different reasons. The complexity of individual experience when not dealt with in public is highlighted and questioned in a bravely critical manner; despite the clear issues it raises with class and privilege, the final night was attended by the Price and Princess of Wales. The Man of Property was the first novel in the famous The Forsyte Saga, a trilogy of novels with an 'interlude' between each one, written between 1906 and 1921. Dealing with the questions of status, class and materialism, The Man of Property introduces us to the Forsyte family, particularly Soames Forsyte, who is acutely aware of his status as 'new money' and equally keen to assert himself as a wealthy man. Jealous of his wife and desperate to own things in order to confirm his wealth to those observing him, he engineers a plan to keep his wife from her friends which backfires spectacularly when, instead of cutting her off, all Soames achieves is enabling her to have an affair. This drives Soames to terrible actions with terrible consequences, which Galsworthy depicts with confidence.

Very typically Edwardian, the novel focuses on conflict between property and art, and to a certain degree much of its emotional power is drawn from Galsworthy's own life, particularly his affair with Ada. Their rendezvous in the countryside of Devon mirror the manner in which Forsyte seeks to relocate his wife and; though theirs was a much healthier relationship, there are clear similarities. By examining the fragile nature of the class system and those moving within it Galsworthy offered an important perspective on the relationships between material wealth, personal happiness and obsession, and the manner in which these change over time. His contemporaries widely regarded the publication of this novel as marking the end of Victorianism. His friend Conrad praised it as "indubitably a piece of art" and, though the notoriously risqué D.H. Lawrence lamented the novel's timidity in the face of sexuality and sensuality, he considered it potentially "a very great novel, a very great satire".

Though he continued to write both plays and novels, it was his work as a playwright for which he was most celebrated by his contemporaries. Indeed, his next novel, The Country House, seems uncharacteristically unfocused, its satirical view of those belonging to the country set comparatively unremarkable and weakly characterised, while at times the tone of satire becomes one of ironic detachment. In 1909 he published Fraternity, an exploration of of the various connections between urban society and the social classes therein, though its representation of lower-class Londoners is utterly unconvincing and ill-informed. Remaining with the subject of the landed gentry and the society surrounding it, in 1915 he published The Freelands, which does not stray far from conservative discussions of capitalism, the rural economy and their interrelationship.

His drama, however, featured a convincingly muted realism, directed at a relatively small, educated and politically-aware audience. His social agenda is prevalent here too, and is represented in a simple and static manner producing arresting instances of high drama. This talent for creating moments of captivating theatre is complimented by an instinctual sense of balance enabling his narratives to vacillate between their emotional high- and low-points, ultimately reaching conclusive equilibrium. This is particularly evident in one of his most popular plays, Strife, published in 1909 and examining the antagonists in a strike at a Cornish tin mine. In this, and in 1910's Justice, he approaches his subject with sympathy, irony and balance, which establishes a position of narrative authority while garnering the audiences trust that he is representing his characters and their motives justly. Justice condemns the use of solitary confinement in prisons, a reformist agenda which caught the liberality of his contemporary audiences along with the home secretary, Winston Churchill. Despite he was careful to disassociate himself with politics and professed himself apolitical, he and his work were nevertheless aligned with the views of the Liberal establishment. He spent much of the duration of the First World War working in a field hospital in France as an orderly having been passed over for military service.

Despite the popularity and brilliance of his work, it was only in 1920 that he had his first true commercial success with The Skin Game, a melodrama dealing with ethics, property and class. The play was adapted by Alfred Hitchcock in 1931. Galsworthy, meanwhile, had turned down a knighthood in 1918, considering his work not sufficient to be made a knight of the realm. He did, however, accept the Belgian Palmes d'Or in the following year. In 1920 he published the second novel in the Forsyte Saga, In Chancery, in which he resumes many of the themes of the first novel, focusing on the marital disharmony between Soames Forsyte and his wife. Katherine Mansfield considered it "a fascinating, brilliant book" in her review in The Atheneum. Then, in 1921, he was elected as the PEN International Literary Club's first president. The concluding novel to The Forsyte Saga, To Let was published in 1921 with a kind of peace being found between Forsyte and his now-ex wife, though he is left contemplating his losses and his greed. More ironic treatment of class confusions followed in Loyalties, bringing with it more popular success which lasted until 1926 and Escape, the last of his popular plays. Though he enjoyed popular success it was inconsistent and relatively small. His Collected Plays was published in 1929.

Over the course of time the appreciation of his work has gradually shifted from his plays to his novels, and particularly the detail and intricacy of his chronicle of English social difference, tension and pretension in The Forsyte Saga. Its success encouraged Galsworthy to revisit Soames Forsyte in a second trilogy, A Modern Comedy, which follows Soames's obsessive love of his daughter Fleur. In its three volumes, The White Monkey (1924), The Silver Spoon (1936) and Swan Song (1928) he examines the English commercial upper-middle class and its ideologies, its instinct to possess as its only way of distinguishing itself manifested in the poisonous materialism of Soames. Interestingly, this emergent social class which he so vehemently criticises is the very class from which he emerged. He witnessed first-hand its insularity, its chauvinism, its restrictive and oppressive morality, its stubborn imperialism and its materialism, and it is this experience which enables him to write so comfortably about it. Swan Song is widely considered among the best of Galsworthy's writing for the depth of its exploration of society and its heightened emotional subtlety. In 1929 he was appointed to the Order of Merit, despite having turned down a knighthood earlier. He spent his last years writing a third trilogy, End of the Chapter, beginning in 1931 with Maid in Waiting, Flowering Wilderness in 1932 and concluding with Over The River in 1933. These are significantly less coherent works and are indicative of his deteriorating health. Indeed, in 1932 he was awarded the Nobel Prize, though he was too ill to attend the ceremony.

Throughout the course of his career he received honorary degrees from the universities of St Andrews (1922), Manchester (1927), Dublin (1929), Cambridge (1930), Sheffield (1930), Oxford (1931), and Princeton (1931). In 1926 New College, Oxford, elected him as an honourary fellow. In photographs he is portrayed as handsome, fastidiously dressed and dignified. He was unusually compassionate and this saw him involved in several charitable and humane causes throughout the course of his life, including penal reforms, attacks on theatrical censorship and campaigning for animal rights. Though he spent the majority of the final seven years of his life at his home in Bury, West Sussex, it was at his home in Hampstead, London, that he died of a brain tumour on 31st January, 1933, six weeks after having been too ill to attend the ceremony in honour of his receiving the Nobel Prize. According to demands made in his will he was cremated and his ashes scattered over the South Downs from an aeroplane. Also in his will was his wish to leave cottages to several of his astonished tenants. He is memorialised in Highgate 'New' Cemetery and in the cloisters of New College, Oxford, where he was an honourary fellow.

www.ingramcontent.com/pod-product-compliance
Lightning Source LLC
Chambersburg PA
CBHW071414170626
46811CB00003B/1404